LETHAL OUTBREAK

FROM THE OUTER REACHES ...

Lethal Outbreak
by Malcolm Rose

Published by Ransom Publishing Ltd.
Unit 7, Brocklands Farm, West Meon, Hampshire GU32 1JN, UK
www.ransom.co.uk

ISBN   978 178127 669 3
First published in 2015

LETHAL OUTBREAK

MALCOLM ROSE

Ransom

BODY HARVEST

When the body of an outer is discovered in the woods, young detective Troy Goodhart and forensic specialist Lexi Iona Four are partnered on the case. Then two more bodies are discovered, and all three corpses are found to have body parts missing. Somebody is killing with a purpose. As major Troy and outer Lexi unpick the case, they enter a complex, dark world of deception, where one false move will mean death.

THE OUTER REACHES

*A world inhabited by two distinct and non-interbreeding humanoid species: **majors** (the majority) and **outers**. The two races are outwardly similar, but they have different talents, different genetics and different body chemistry.*

In this world, meet major Troy Goodhart and outer Lexi Iona Four. They make an amazing crime-fighting partnership.

SCENE 1

Monday 14th April, Afternoon

On the other side of the thickened glass, three lifeless bodies in sky-blue overalls lay on the floor of the high-security laboratory. They looked like astronauts who had been exposed to lethal alien air. On the wall above them, a red light glared with the warning: *EXIT LABORATORY*. Two detectives – Troy Goodhart and Lexi Iona Four – stood outside helplessly, unable to enter and examine the bodies in case the sealed lab was contaminated with poison.

'So,' Troy said, 'to go in, we'd have to dress up in all that space-suit gear?'

Lexi was an outer and, like most outers, she had a talent for science and technology. 'They're called positive-pressure protective suits, or PPPS, but they're usually known as moon suits or blue suits – and, yes, sometimes space suits. They cover you completely and they're airtight.'

'How do you breathe in them?'

'This is a Biosafety Level 4 lab. The most secure there is.' Lexi pointed to the ceiling of the room. 'If you're working inside, you get fresh air through that tubing – see it dangling down? Everyone in there has an air tube sealed into their suits. It's their own private life support system and it's there so nothing in the lab comes into contact with them. Not even the air.'

Troy was a major. He wasn't so skilled in science but he had an instinct for people and the things that they did. 'How do you take a drink? Or go to the loo?'

'You don't,' Lexi replied. 'It's not easy work in there, weighed down by all the gear, getting hot and sweaty, not able to take a drink or even scratch an itch. And all the time you're wondering if you're going to slip and puncture the suit. That's pretty much a death sentence. Requires a lot of concentration. Very tiring. So, they don't do long shifts. They come out after a while. That's when they visit the toilet.'

Both of the detectives were sixteen years old and they had been a team for just one week. Investigating the deaths in the BSL4 laboratory was their second case.

'If the idea is to stop anything getting out of the lab – any poisons or fatal bugs or whatever,' Troy said, 'they can't just open a door and walk out when they want to go.'

Lexi smiled. 'No. It's a bit more complicated than that. They've got to be decontaminated before they can leave. On the way in and the way out, they go through a few showers – one's a quick-drench disinfectant – and a vacuum room where all the air gets pumped out.'

'An airlock like you see in spaceships? In science fiction films?'

'Usually more than one. There's a room that blasts you with ultraviolet light as well. That's to kill any biohazards, like nasty microorganisms. There might be a section that fills with killer fumes as well. Sometimes there are even more safety steps. In some labs like this, they come out two at a time so they can scrub each other's suits down with disinfectant. All the doors are electronically controlled to make sure only one can open at a time. If two or more opened together, it'd be a security breach.'

'That fits.' Pointing to the right, Troy said, 'There's a sink in all three cabinets over there. That means water. And cages – with dead mice in them. So, there's air, equipment, animals and food. What happens about all that?'

'Everything that goes in or out – including air and water – goes through much the same decontamination. Equipment and clothing is steam-cleaned at 130 degrees to kill off any nasties. The whole thing's designed to stop accidental release of whatever dangerous stuff they're handling.'

'Have you ever worked anywhere like this?' Troy asked.

'No, but I learned all about it. There's quite a lot of training just to go in and come out safely.'

Troy gazed sadly at the three scientists sprawled on the floor. 'But something can still go wrong.'

'Looks like it. They've got microphones – so they can talk to each other and to their supervisor who monitors their life signs from out here.'

Troy sighed. 'And there hasn't been any chat – or life signs – since this morning.'

'That's what the supervisor said.'

'Why are we here? Isn't this just an accident? A horrible accident.'

'Maybe,' Lexi replied. 'But these people are

brilliant at handling dangerous stuff. They don't have a lot of accidents.'

'How about equipment failure?'

'I think you'll find the people who make BSL4 systems are pretty brilliant as well.'

'And if it wasn't an accident … '

'Yeah,' said Lexi. 'It was something else, like sabotage and murder.'

'These weird blue suits. Why are they called positive pressure?'

'They're pumped up like a tyre. Only nowhere near as much. If the suit's punctured, air blows out instead of getting sucked in. It gives the scientist wearing it a bit of protection against the damage.'

'A *bit* of protection,' Troy murmured.

'A slow stream of air isn't perfect. And if it deflates completely … that's that.'

'Time to see the lab supervisor and unit director.' Nodding towards the victims, Troy said, 'We need to find out who they are, what they were working on and what we do about them.'

SCENE 2

Monday 14th April, Late afternoon

Shallow End Laboratories carried out scientific research for The National Space Centre, and the whole unit was managed by a middle-aged major called Saul Tingle. Troy and Lexi stood in front of him as he sat behind his huge desk. To the side, the victims' laboratory supervisor slumped against the wall, her elbow resting on a shelf.

'It's all very regrettable and ... embarrassing,' Saul admitted to the detectives. 'Our thoughts at this difficult time are with our colleagues. They were all outers, so they didn't have families. No one to offer our sympathies to. Even so … it's a great loss.'

His words sounded sincere, but Troy detected annoyance in the man's body language. He also sensed that the unit director was trying to cover up nervousness. 'Who were they?' Troy asked.

Saul waved towards the lab supervisor and Troy suspected that the gesture meant he didn't know the names of the victims.

Clearly upset, Julia Neve Nineteen said, 'Konnie Marina Five, Brandon Kane Six and Tyla Sorrel Three.' She paused before muttering, 'My friends, as well as work colleagues.'

'I'm sorry,' Troy said. 'What were they working on?'

'I'm a manager and director,' Saul replied. 'I'm not a qualified scientist so I let my staff deal with the nitty-gritty science, but let me say this. You're probably aware that a Mars probe returned to Earth a few weeks ago. It was all over the news. It brought back a Martian soil sample. We call it SUMP, short for Substance Unknown from Mars Probe.'

Julia Nineteen took up the story. 'Before we try to identify all the substances in it, we had to make sure it's safe to be allowed in our atmosphere.'

'In your highest security lab?'

Julia said, 'We always handle alien material with unknown toxicity at containment level four, until we've found out if we need to carry on working at that level or if we can safely drop down to lower security.'

Butting in, Saul said, 'It's very important you understand we take every possible safety measure. This is our protocol. Dangerous alien substances that carry a high risk of infection are always contained within BSL4. It's the same for Earthly microorganisms if they cause serious-to-fatal disease and there's no cure or vaccine available. Because we're ultra-cautious, all unknowns and suspected biological hazards get the highest security treatment until we test how harmful they are and find they don't merit it.'

'That figures,' Troy replied. 'And what was the result on SUMP?'

'It wasn't good news,' Julia answered. 'Something in it kills mice and a lot of other lab animals we tested. It also kills outer cells – but not major cells – very quickly and very efficiently. That's why we were still working under BSL4 conditions. We were trying to identify the toxic component.'

'So you think the cause of death is this poisonous soil from Mars.'

'It's obvious, isn't it?'

'But if I went in, I could ignore all the safety stuff because I'm a major and the poison wouldn't affect me. Is that what you're saying? I could just walk in there and sort it out?'

'Yes and no,' Julia Nineteen replied. 'Obviously we can't put a living major at risk by exposing one to SUMP, but we know cells from majors aren't affected. So, if you got contaminated, as far as we know, you'd be fine. But if you brought the slightest amount out – which would be unavoidable – I'd drop, along with every other outer. Somehow, it blocks our metabolism. In other words, it stops the chemical reactions in our cells. It stops outer life.'

'There's something else you need to appreciate,' Saul said. 'If the toxic ingredient's a bacterium that's evolved in the extreme extra-terrestrial conditions on Mars, it must be very hardy indeed. If it was ever released into our milder environment, it'd spread like wildfire and we wouldn't have the tools to stop it. If it can survive on Mars, it can probably survive any antibiotics we throw at it.'

Troy shivered. 'An outbreak would be lethal to half of humanity?'

'Almost certainly,' said Saul. 'Now you know why we're so careful. All work with biohazards like SUMP

– or materials of unknown toxicity – is confined to Class 3 safety cabinets within the BSL4 lab.'

'So,' Troy asked, 'have I got this right? If your people were killed by Martian soil, the poisonous part must have escaped from a safety cabinet and into the lab air. But that wouldn't affect them unless all three had faulty space suits as well.'

'That's right.'

'When there's a lot of smoke, there's almost always a fire.'

'Pardon?'

'Faulty cabinets and faulty suits. It's too much of a coincidence to be an accident.' Troy glanced at Lexi and took a deep breath before turning towards the laboratory supervisor. 'Your three colleagues. Konnie, Brandon and Tyla. Do they grab any available protective suit to go in the lab or do they have their own?'

'They're personalized,' Julia said. 'They're highly specialized, made to fit each individual worker. There's a little identifier on the chest. Mine's got JN19 written on it.'

'Who looks after them?'

'We all tend to look after our own,' she replied. 'I'm told that other people who rely on a bit of cloth to save their lives – skydivers – always pack their own parachutes. They want to make sure it's done right. We're the same. And there's a sort of ritual we go through after we come out. We all do it. We take off one of our gloves, blow it up like a balloon and watch it for a few seconds. Believe me, after you've been working in BSL4 with hypodermic syringes and needles, you're delighted to see the glove doesn't go down. It means you haven't had a puncture.'

'Do they check the suits are okay before they go in?'

Julia nodded. 'There's a routine.'

'I understand all the safety stages they go through on the way out,' said Troy. 'But why do they do the same thing on the way in?'

'It's not just a case of protecting the planet from alien samples,' she told him. 'The lab's also got to protect any alien matter from Earthly contamination.'

'Okay. That fits. When your workmates died, you were supervising them?'

Julia looked away in anguish for a moment. 'Yes.'

'So, what happened?'

The lab supervisor was in her late thirties, Troy guessed, but right now she looked haggard and older. 'I don't watch them all the time,' she said.

'But did they say something had gone wrong?'

Julia's distraught face reddened with shame. She

glanced momentarily at Saul and said, 'We're short-staffed. Sometimes, I get called away from the control room to another job.'

'Did that happen this morning?'

'It's usually fine,' she spluttered. 'They're professionals. They know what they're doing. They don't need me breathing down their necks all the time. It was only for a few minutes. I wish ... But it's too late now.'

'So, no one saw or heard what happened to them at the vital moment?'

Saul put his head in his hands when Julia muttered, 'No.'

'Does the control room record video?'

'No, it's just a monitor, like a window on the laboratory.'

'Could anyone have sneaked into the lab and tampered with the equipment?'

Saul answered, 'Access to BSL4 is strictly controlled by the laboratory supervisor.'

Troy looked at Julia Nineteen. 'I'll need a list of everyone who's ever been inside – and when.'

'I'll send it to your life-logger.'

'Is there any chance anyone else went in this morning when you weren't watching?'

'No,' Julia replied. 'There wasn't enough time.

Anyway, one thing the system does log is the doors opening and closing. Today, only one lot of people went in.' Her voice reduced to a croaky whisper as she added, 'And none came out.'

'Who called you away from the control room – and why?'

'An animal handler called Eric Kiss.'

'You didn't say why.'

Julia hesitated. 'I'd rather talk to you in private about that.'

'All right. Later.' Changing the subject, Troy asked, 'Why is there a red warning light on in the lab?'

'It's telling them they've been inside too long.'

'Okay,' Troy said. 'I need some help here. We've got to examine them and a pathologist needs to check how they died. How are we going to do that without killing every outer around?'

'We've discussed this,' Saul replied. 'There's an emergency protocol for cleaning the lab in the event of a contamination event, but you're not going to like it. None of us will.'

'What is it?'

'We can steam-clean it, suck all the air out, fumigate it and then pump it full of a highly corrosive liquid that'll destroy any remaining organic matter.'

'Including the evidence?'

'Yes. Including the blue suits and most of the flesh on the bodies.'

'No,' Lexi said.

'We don't have a choice,' Saul replied. 'Sooner rather than later, we've got to decontaminate the lab.'

'After we've done a post-mortem,' Lexi insisted.

Saul shook his head. 'It's too risky. I can't have amateurs in BSL4. My scientists go through extensive training in handling extremely hazardous agents. They have to get to grips with all the containment functions of the lab and its equipment, understand the design features, and learn how to manipulate small vials, syringes and so on whilst wearing a blue suit. When their hands are inside a safety cabinet, they'll be wearing two sets of gloves. Acquiring all those skills isn't easy or fast.'

'Your people are experts in what they do,' Lexi said. 'But I'm expert in deciding if this is murder and, if it is, getting the most out of the crime scene. I need your cooperation to let me do my job.'

'I have a greater responsibility to the planet – and every outer on it. I have to make sure we're safe from a deadly alien infection.'

Lexi glanced towards Julia and then asked the unit director, 'What if one of your experts volunteered to come in with me?'

Saul took a deep breath as he thought about it. 'We could get you into some gear, I suppose, and take you in so you can do a visual examination. You could tell a volunteer what to do on your behalf, but you can't bring out any samples. No clothing, no tissue, nothing. Not even your life-logger.'

'It's better than nothing. It'd be me and Crime Central's pathologist, Kofi Seven.'

Saul sighed. 'It's very much against my better judgement.'

'But it's a deal. All we need is … ' Again Lexi looked at the laboratory supervisor.

'Yes, I'll do it,' said Julia.

'Okay,' Saul replied reluctantly. 'But straight after, I'm going to begin the emergency decontamination procedure. I'm not delaying any more.'

SCENE 3

Through the loudspeaker, Julia's voice explained, 'Unlike the positive-pressure suits, the whole lab's under negative pressure – a slight vacuum. That means if there was a leak – not that we've ever had one – outside air would get sucked in rather than inside air that could be contaminated leaking out.'

Actually, she was talking to Lexi and Kofi, as two technicians helped them into their positive-pressure protective suits. Troy was eavesdropping in the observation and control room. He could also watch what was happening on a large screen. When all three of them were totally sealed inside their suits, Troy listened as they used their microphones to keep in contact with each other. He could hear their breathing as if they were in the same room and uncomfortably close to his ears. The effect reminded him of a rasping TV commentary from an underwater scuba diver.

The two technicians came into the same room, sat at the controls and announced into a microphone that they were ready.

'Okay,' Julia said. 'They're going to shut off your air supply for a few seconds and increase the pressure of your suits. You'll hear a strange hissing noise and it'll feel like you're being squeezed all over. Your ears will feel the extra pressure most. It's part of the procedure to check there's no punctures. Here we go. Hold your breath.'

After ten seconds, one of the technicians said, 'All three suits intact and holding pressure. Air back on. You're free to get started.'

'Thanks, guys,' Julia replied. 'That's Blaine and Fern,' she told her two new companions. 'They're looking after us for the duration. From now on you have to remember we're going into enemy territory. Deadly territory. You don't get impatient and you don't rush. Blaine and Fern aren't going anywhere. It doesn't matter how long it takes. The procedure's in place to keep us all safe, so we put up with it. Before we go into each chamber, we have to disconnect our air supply from one place and then reconnect it in the next. It's simple. Just follow what I do. First door opening. This is where you get drenched – on the outside, that is. It's a very powerful power shower. Just stand up straight, arms and legs spread out, and let the disinfectant do its job.'

When it came, Troy heard the clatter on their suits like hail on a roof.

'Next we're going to be dried off, put under vacuum and bathed in ultraviolet light. It's okay. Your visors have got a uv filter. You won't get blinded.'

Blaine Twenty-Two leaned towards his colleague and, out of range of the microphone, whispered, 'The girl – Lexi – she's amazingly cool under the circumstances.'

With a smile, Fern replied, 'Not like the pathologist, as it turns out. His heart rate's increased. He's sweating as well, but he's within normal range. He's not exactly enjoying himself, though.'

The whole screen turned bright blue as ultraviolet light enveloped the three cloaked figures, killing off any remaining germs.

Troy jumped out of his chair and said, 'What was that?'

'A burst of uv, that's all,' said Fern.

'No. I mean, there was a mark on the heel of … I don't know who's who. The person on the right.'

'That's Julia,' Blaine said. 'What sort of mark?'

'It was a darker blue patch on the back of her left heel. Didn't you see it?'

Both technicians shook their heads blankly.

'If you're both outers, I've got better eyesight. A slightly wider range of wavelengths. Maybe that's why … '

'As it happens, I'm a major,' Fern Mountstephen said.

'Didn't you see it?'

'No, but I have to say I wasn't staring at anyone's heel. I was monitoring life signs.'

Worried, Troy watched the screen, where it seemed that three astronauts were taking ungainly steps on another planet. In reality, they were only a few metres away from the control room but it could have been another world. A dangerous world. 'Any chance of them repeating the ultraviolet stage so we can see it again?' Troy asked nervously.

'No. They're going through to the fumigation chamber. The last one before they enter the lab.'

'So, any second now, it'll be too late to recall them?'

'Yes,' Fern answered.

'And if there's a fault in Julia's suit … ?'

'We're not getting any negative feedback,' Blaine said. 'Everything's normal and intact. All systems green.'

'But I'm giving you feedback. I'm telling you what I saw. Something weird.'

'It was probably just something harmless sticking to the PPPS.'

'After a power shower and everything?'

The two technicians glanced at each other.

Blaine said, 'If there was an issue, the system would register it as a problem.'

Fern announced, 'Fumigation nearing completion.'

Troy shook his head. 'I think you should recall them before it's too late.'

'On what grounds?'

Troy hesitated, his heart beating far too fast. 'When you're dealing with something unknown, you assume the worst. That's how you work. I think you should assume the worst here as well.'

'When you get this far into the system,' Blaine said, waving towards the monitor, 'you don't want to be called back on a whim. It's so long-winded and stressful. They won't thank us.'

'You've already had three die in there today. Why

take the chance? Maybe *they* had something wrong with the backs of their heels as well.'

'That's a bit far-fetched.'

Troy watched Lexi, Kofi and Julia detach their air supplies and shuffle forward, waiting for the door to the lab to open.

'No!' Troy shouted. 'Blame me, but get them out of there. Something's not right!'

Blaine threw up his hands. 'Okay. It's your call. They're going in for your investigation, not our research.' He leaned towards the microphone. 'Sorry about this. I've locked the door. Detective Goodhart wants you back out. He thinks something's wrong with your suit, Julia. We need an inspection.'

Julia groaned. Her voice said, 'Are any of the monitors telling you I'm compromised?'

'No.'

'So, what did he see?'

'A patch of colour on your left heel. Only under uv lamps, apparently.'

'Did you see anything?'

'No. Maybe it's not visible to outers.'

'Did you see it, Fern?'

'No. But, to be fair, I wasn't really looking.'

'Was there anything on the other two suits?'

The technicians both glanced over their shoulders at Troy. He shook his head.

'No,' Blaine said into the microphone. 'Do you want to override his decision?'

The breathy sound from the loudspeaker became a sigh. After five seconds, Julia replied, 'No. It's his show, after all. We're coming out.'

They had not gone into the high-security lab, so they didn't need to decontaminate themselves on the way out. Even so, they had to traipse back through each compartment. When the three cumbersome figures finally emerged from the last stage, Fern turned to Blaine and pointed at one monitor. 'Look!'

The green light above the screen turned bright red and a siren sounded.

Astonished, Blaine and Fern both turned towards Troy. Above the noise of the alarm, Blaine said, 'Julia's moon suit's not maintaining pressure. It's got a leak!'

'Which means … ?'

'You just saved her life.'

SCENE 4

Monday 14th April, Evening

Lexi had taken over a corner of Shallow End
Laboratories to perform an analysis of the remains of
the sticky tape that had been firmly attached to the
left heel of Julia Nineteen's blue suit. She shone
radiation from a hand-held ultraviolet lamp on the
cloth and looked quizzically at Troy.

He nodded. 'Yes. It's faded and not much left, but
I can still see it's a deeper blue.'

Julia shrugged. 'I can't.'

Lexi smiled, 'Nor me, but I know what's happened
– and it's sheer genius. Cunning. When ultraviolet

light falls on the tape – on the way into the lab – it reacts. It releases an acid. I don't know which yet, but it attacks the tape itself and the cloth underneath. Slowly.'

'You're thinking the same stuff was on Konnie's, Brandon's and Tyla's?' said Troy.

'Yeah. None of them would have seen the colour development – even if they were looking at the back of each other's heels – because it's beyond an outer's visual range. The reaction produces a small amount of corrosive goo that takes minutes to eat through the material. Hey presto, the suit would be registering as fine when they went into the hot zone. That means – if it's any consolation, Julia – you couldn't have done anything to save them. By the time they'd gone into the lab, apparently protected perfectly well, the acid would have already begun to make a small hole.'

The lab supervisor did not look comforted. 'Forgive me if I don't share your enthusiasm for how my friends were killed.'

'Sorry,' said Lexi. 'But you've got to admit it's really clever chemistry. The hole would get bigger until the positive pressure wasn't enough to keep the poison out.' She hesitated before adding, 'And that's it. There's nothing else for me to analyse on the material. The power showers have removed any fingerprints, fibres or DNA.'

As always, Troy's mind was racing. He shook his head.

'What's up?' Lexi prompted.

'Why sabotage only four named suits? The ones you and Kofi used were fine.'

'We checked,' Julia said. 'None of the reserve suits had been tampered with. The other named suits were okay as well.'

'Whoever did it was after four specific people,' Troy deduced.

'Or he just went for the suits that were the most used,' Julia suggested. 'That'd be the four of us.'

'There's something else, though,' said Troy, still puzzled. 'Having a hole in your suit isn't good, but it's not enough to make you die. If SUMP had been where it was supposed to be – inside a sealed safety cabinet – it wouldn't have come into contact with them. No deaths.'

Julia didn't reply. She simply nodded.

'The lab was sabotaged as well,' said Lexi.

Troy agreed. 'Someone let SUMP out of the bag.'

'We're not going to find out now,' Julia said. 'Saul's about to start the emergency protocol and that'll destroy the evidence. He won't let anyone in because he doesn't trust the suits any more.'

Struck by a thought, Lexi shook her head. 'There is a way. I'll get onto Terabyte and the technical crew. We're going to send in a drone.'

SCENE 5

The drone looked like a child's toy, like a miniature helicopter, no bigger than thirty centimetres in any direction. But it was much more sophisticated than any toy. It could be manoeuvred precisely and its cameras had super-high resolution. It couldn't carry out a post-mortem on the victims like Kofi Seven but, under the circumstances, it was the best option for extracting information from a crime scene that was tantalisingly close yet inaccessible. Of course, the remote-control device was sacrificial. Once it had beamed its pictures to Troy and Lexi, it would remain in the BSL4 lab for the decontamination process. Crime Central would be able to salvage it only after it had been exposed to the highly corrosive fluid that would destroy any living and organic matter.

The drone had been designed originally to take detailed aerial photographs and collect air samples from hard-to-reach places. Lexi would have loved to analyse a sample of the air from the BSL4 lab, but the risk was far too great. She would have to be content with the robot's high-quality imaging capability.

Lexi, Troy and Julia sat in front of the screen in the control room while Terabyte – the best computer geek in Crime Central – operated the flying drone. 'Is this the last door?' Terabyte asked, as he allowed the drone to hover in the fumigation room.

'Yes,' Julia told him. 'Vacuum on to clear the fumes.' After a few seconds, she reported, 'Returning to atmospheric pressure now.' She flicked a switch. 'Door to BSL4 opening.'

Terabyte drove the drone forward into the toxic environment. As a machine, it was immune to any poisons in the air and it didn't need a PPPS. 'Where do you want it?'

'The nearest body,' Lexi replied. 'I want a close-up of the back of the heel.'

'Which heel?' Terabyte asked.

'Both.'

The drone hovered a few centimetres over the body nearest to the door and zoomed in on Konnie Five's right heel. Showing off the device's camera, Terabyte said, 'Do you want to see the whole of the heel or an individual thread?'

'I just want to see if the material's damaged.'

'There's your answer,' said Terabyte.

On the monitor, the clarity of the image was amazing. The protective material had disintegrated over an area of two or three square centimetres. Some small fragments of shiny tape were still adhering around the edges of the hole.

Lexi nodded. 'That's how the poison sneaked in, then. Don't bother with her other heel. There's no point looking for anything else on the rest of her suit either. It'll be spotless after the treatment on the way in. Move on to the next body.'

It was Tyla Three, and the back of her right heel was flat against the floor. The drone was able to focus only on her left heel and it showed the same damage: an almost rectangular flaw with corroded fabric and flecks of tape around it.

Both of Brandon Six's heels were in view and his left had been sabotaged.

'You are recording all this, aren't you?' Lexi asked.

'Of course,' Terabyte answered. 'What else?'

'I want to look at the safety cabinets,' Troy said. 'Is one of them damaged? Is there any evidence of SUMP getting out?'

'SUMP?' Terabyte queried.

'Substance unknown – and very poisonous – from Mars probe.'

'Cool,' he muttered as he manoeuvred the drone towards the first sealed unit. 'Are you two specializing in crazy cases?'

Under Terabyte's command, the drone's camera scanned the enclosed transparent compartment. Heavy-duty gloves were fixed into the front of the unit, so that one of the scientists could place their already gloved hands into them and work on something hazardous inside the compartment without ever breaking containment.

'Does it look okay, Julia?' Troy asked. 'Nothing unusual or broken?'

'No, it looks fine. Zoom in on the gloves. They're the only weak point.'

But after a thorough close-up inspection, Julia did not spot any damage.

'No,' she said. 'Everything's as it should be.'

'Move on to the next one,' Troy said to Terabyte.

Carefully and slowly, the drone glided back and

forth, photographing every part of the glass-fronted cupboard. The fine images allowed them all to examine its exterior and, because of the transparent pane, its contents. There were several pieces of equipment lying on the spotless work surface, a lot of animal corpses – mostly mice and white rats – in cages, and bottles of chemicals, both solids and liquids.

'That's the same,' Julia told them. 'Nothing out of place. The seals are fine and I can't see any tears in the built-in gloves.'

Troy sighed. He was about to ask Terabyte to scan the final safety cabinet but the drone was already on its way across the laboratory. This time, Terabyte started the imaging at the top of the compartment and moved the drone from side-to-side as it descended.

Troy didn't see any faults, cracks or holes. When he glanced towards Julia, he also realized from her expression that she hadn't noticed anything that could cause a leak either. He sighed. If there were no defects, how had SUMP polluted the laboratory, worked its way inside the scientists' blue suits and killed them?

Abruptly, Julia leapt to her feet. 'Hang on. The vial of SUMP has gone!'

'What?'

Her face had turned white. 'There's a bottle of it in each cabinet. At least, there should be. The other two had their vials. I saw them. But the one from here is missing!'

'Are you sure?'

'Of course I'm sure,' she snapped.

'Photograph every surface, Terabyte,' Lexi said. 'In case it's on the floor or somewhere else in there.'

'Okay,' he replied. 'But if one of these bodies is lying on it … ' He shrugged. 'No go.'

'How much soil would be in it?' Troy asked.

Stunned, Julia replied, 'A little less than five grams. Easily enough to wipe out every outer on Earth, I should think.'

SCENE 6

Tuesday 15th April, Morning

Troy watched as both Lexi and Julia Nineteen guzzled beer for breakfast. As a major, he didn't drink alcohol because it would quickly intoxicate him. Outers didn't have the same metabolism and they knocked it back without a care. Out of the window, Troy could see a solitary crane on the skyline. It was putting the finishing touches to the sports stadium that would host the coming Integrated Games.

In the early hours, the high-security lab had been thoroughly cleaned, disinfected and fumigated by Saul Tingle's emergency protocol.

'Our forensic team's been through the lab,' Lexi said to Julia. 'Nothing useful's left. It's like it's been scorched. Glass vials would have survived, though. But there were only two. No sign of the third, whole or in pieces.'

Julia took a deep breath. 'That's what I feared.'

'It means the motive might have been to get hold of some Martian soil,' Troy said. 'Have you ever heard of anyone wanting to do that?'

'No. It'd be … suicidal.'

'For an outer,' Troy remarked. 'Any ideas why someone might want it?'

'No.' She put down her beer. 'Unless they had some sort of grudge against outers. Or scientists. Or the work we do here.'

'Mmm. Why would anyone think like that?'

'I don't know,' she replied.

'Well, my guess is someone grabbed the third vial, sprinkled enough SUMP around the lab to kill the next lot of scientists to go in, and took the rest,' Troy said. 'The same person who sabotaged the blue suits. But even if we've got no idea where the poison is and who's got it, at least we know it's safely sealed. Because outers aren't dropping like flies.'

Lexi grimaced. 'For how long?' She took another swig of beer.

Troy tapped his life-logger. 'Thanks for the list of everyone who's been in the BSL4 lab,' he said to Julia. 'There's a lot of them. I notice it includes Saul Tingle and Eric Kiss. Tell me about Eric.'

'Yes. He's one of the guys who look after laboratory animals. That's why he needs access to all our labs. He sets up the live tests on toxicity.'

Troy nodded. 'But there's more to it than that.'

'Yes,' Julia admitted. 'I didn't want to talk about it in front of Saul.' She glanced around furtively before continuing. 'It's a bit embarrassing really. We're … friends.'

'What?' Lexi exclaimed. 'With that name, he must be a major.'

'Yes,' she replied, as if ashamed.

Troy didn't react with the same distaste as Lexi. He was trained to get the most out of witnesses. Making it obvious that her friendship was peculiar did not help. He preferred sympathy. He shrugged. 'I understand,' he said, even though he didn't. 'But, to be clear, when you say friendship … ?'

Julia looked lost for words.

'Lexi and I are workmates, even friends most of the time,' Troy said with a grin. 'But you mean something north of that.'

'People won't call it love. We're two separate species.'

'People mean different things when they talk about loving this and that, him or her,' Troy replied. 'So, the important thing is, what do *you* call it?'

Head bowed, Julia said, 'I think we love each other, yes.'

Out of Julia's sight, Lexi pulled a face, as if she had a horrible taste in her mouth.

'And yesterday you had a few minutes together for what?' Troy asked.

'He was upset about something he'd heard. Rumours. You won't tell Saul Tingle about this, will you?'

'We only share our findings with those who need to know. There's no reason for your manager to be in on it.'

'But you'll interview Eric?'

'Yes,' Troy replied. 'He's been to the crime scene and he called you away at the vital moment. That makes him a suspect.'

Julia sighed but she also nodded.

'We'll do it now,' Troy told her. Smiling, he added, 'Before you can warn him we're on our way.' At the door, he hesitated and said, 'One more thing.'

'Yes?'

'Before yesterday morning, when was the last time someone worked in the BSL4 lab?'

'That'd be a maintenance crew on Friday afternoon.'

'The control room keeps a record of the doors opening and closing. So, what about the weekend? Did someone go in – and come out – between Friday afternoon and yesterday morning? That must be when the vial disappeared and the lab got contaminated. Unless it was down to the last engineer to leave on Friday.'

'I'll check all that and let you know.'

'Thanks. And remember, one of the sabotaged suits was yours. You were a target. So, if you want a uniformed police guard, we can arrange it.'

'I don't think ... No.'

'All right. Take care. Double check everything if you do any risky jobs.'

'Thanks.'

Walking towards the Animal Section, Lexi complained, 'An outer and a major. It's not natural.'

'When I was little, my grandma had this scruffy little dog and she used to say how much she loved him.' Troy shrugged. 'Chalk and cheese species.'

'Huh. That's different.'

'I didn't think we were here to make judgements on people's lifestyles.'

'Even so … ' Lexi shuddered. Lowering her voice, she added, 'It might be relevant to the case, though. This major – Eric Kiss – could be using Julia. Maybe he got involved with her so he could distract her.'

'Yeah. I used that with Julia as an excuse for questioning him, but the bad guy wouldn't have had to distract her. Even if she'd been glued to the monitor, she wouldn't have seen the sticky-tape tactic and she wouldn't have been able to do anything about it. And it's obvious Eric Kiss doesn't have a grudge against outers in general, because he struck up a relationship with one.'

'If it's genuine,' Lexi muttered. She pushed open the door of the animal department and, trying to lift her mood, she said, 'I've always fancied being a zoo keeper, working with lions, tigers, sharks and snakes.'

Troy laughed. 'You always fancy anything dangerous.'

'An element of risk always makes things exciting. It's called adrenalin.'

Eric Kiss was bound to be a disappointment to Lexi. He mostly handled mice and rats, preparing them for scientific experiments. The greatest risk seemed to be a nip on the finger from an ill-tempered rodent. He was much taller and broader than Julia, and a few years younger.

'Have you spoken to Julia in the last few minutes?' Troy asked him.

'No.' He put down a bowl of animal feed and turned towards Troy. 'Last time we were together was last night. She told me about yesterday. I mean, when she nearly went into the lab. You stopped her. I just wanted to say we're both grateful. Very grateful. Maybe she didn't thank you directly. I think she's in shock for her friends.'

Troy shrugged. He wasn't yet sure whether Eric was sincere or whether he was trying to create a good impression because he thought a nice person wouldn't be a murder suspect. 'Any major would have done the same.'

'I know what you're getting at. I have a relationship with Julia that most people would regard as bizarre.'

'That's not what I was getting at. I was thinking about a major having a wider visual range. That's all. Your relationship doesn't bother me and it's not illegal, so it's none of my business. I'm more interested in why you spoke to her yesterday morning.'

'I feel … guilty for calling her away,' Eric said. 'I shouldn't have … '

'Why did you?'

'Not everyone's as understanding and enlightened as you. Some people don't think we should … spend time together. They talk behind our backs. Some might even threaten us.'

'Threaten?'

'I wanted to speak to her because I'd got wind of people plotting, threatening to get us sacked. It seems we make some feel uncomfortable.'

'Who?'

Next to Eric's shoulder, a mouse suddenly scrabbled at its cage. It was probably impatient for food.

'A friend of mine overheard a conversation or two. I shouldn't accuse anyone on flimsy grounds … '

'Like they accuse you and Julia on flimsy grounds?'

Eric smiled sadly. 'I don't want to sink to the same depths and I don't want to speak ill of the dead, but Brandon Six got told and didn't approve. Neither did Fern Mountstephen. And Precious Austin was quite militant about it weeks ago.'

'Who's Precious Austin?'

'One of the engineers.'

Troy nodded. 'Ah, yes.' She was on the list of staff who'd been trained to work in the BSL4 lab. 'Rumours are like fuel on a wildfire,' he said. 'They spread like crazy. I'm surprised there's anyone around here who doesn't know about the two of you.'

'We're still in the denial and damage limitation phase.'

'When were you last in the BSL4 lab?'

'Thursday. Setting up some toxicity tests. I was due back in yesterday afternoon but … events transpired against it. Tragically.'

Troy glanced around the room. 'You don't object to using animals in research.'

'Not at all. They're a lower life form.'

'And you don't have a grudge against outers in general?'

'No.' He smiled and added, 'Definitely not a lower life form.'

'Do you hold a grudge against the people who are whispering about you and Julia – like Brandon Six?'

Eric looked horrified. 'It disappoints me. It doesn't make me angry. Certainly not enough to kill someone – alongside two perfectly innocent colleagues. And you'd have to ask yourself why I'd sabotage my best friend's moon suit.'

'What makes you think the protective suits were interfered with?'

'Julia,' he answered without hesitation. 'She told me last night.'

It was the response that Troy expected. 'That's it for now.' Nodding towards the rows of cages and smiling wryly, he said, 'The rats are getting restless.'

'I can deal with the ones in here. The ones out there,' Eric said, waving towards the door, 'are more troublesome.'

Troy nodded. 'Good luck with Julia.'

As they went back down the corridor, Lexi muttered, 'Creepy.'

Troy glanced at his partner. He saw puzzlement, not hatred, on her face. 'Well, I thought he was open and genuine. Bad guys don't usually talk so much. They don't volunteer information like he did. You have to squeeze it out of them.'

'Maybe he's a very clever bad guy.'

Troy laughed. 'Maybe. I'm not ruling him out on a feeling.'

SCENE 7

Sitting inside The Hungry Human, Lexi pulled another face. 'But why's it called a hot dog? You majors eat some funny stuff – lots of things you don't know what's inside – but a hot dog?'

'Do you want a sample for DNA profiling?'

'Just tell me.' She bit into her fly larvae pizza.

'Well … ' He hesitated.

'Ha. It's another one you don't have a clue about. Like sausages. There could be anything in there. Pig, horse, even dog.'

'I would've had a clue,' Troy replied with a grin. 'I

offered you some DNA but you refused.'

The Hungry Human was one of many diners with a menu that featured major and outer meals, so it attracted customers from both human races.

Lexi looked up from her life-logger. 'It says here a hot dog is basically processed meat, fat, salt, garlic and other gruesome bits and pieces. The meat trimmings are usually pork and beef but sometimes it's cheaper mush – chicken or turkey. Not what you'd call health food.' She paused before adding, 'Listen. "The suspicion that hot dogs sometimes contain dog meat is only occasionally vindicated."'

Feeling the vibrations from his own life-logger, Troy put down his lunch, drenched with tomato ketchup, and checked the incoming message. It was from Julia Nineteen. Keeping his voice down, he read it aloud to Lexi. 'The end-of-the-week maintenance crew was Fern Mountstephen and Blaine Twenty-Two. You met them both yesterday. They went in together and left together. More interesting, someone went into BSL4 on Sunday. Not an officially sanctioned visit. This person – or more than one person – went in at eight o'clock in the evening and came out half an hour later.'

Lexi nodded. 'Useful. Very useful.'

'In more ways than one.'

'How do you mean?'
'It's stopped you going on about my hot dog.'

SCENE 8

It was going to be a long afternoon. At Troy's request, Saul Tingle had given them use of an interview room within Shallow End Laboratories. Troy wanted to talk to everyone who was permitted entry to BSL4. All of them would have the skills needed to handle a vial of SUMP safely. Really, Troy had only one significant question for each of them. He wanted to know who had an alibi for Sunday evening and who didn't.

While the parade of staff passed through the room, he and Lexi also checked who had the expertise to make sticky tape that released acid when ultraviolet light fell on it.

They began at the top – with the unit director. Saul Tingle almost exploded with indignation. 'You're asking me if I went into the secure lab? But I'm the boss. And I'm not a scientist. I don't think I'm a suspect either.'

'That's where we don't agree,' said Troy. 'I think everyone on this list – trained to go into the high-security lab – is a suspect.'

'But … '

Troy interrupted. 'The thing is, who's a suspect and who isn't is *our* choice, not yours.'

Saul wiped away a drop of sweat from his forehead and sighed heavily. 'I only went through training to see what it was like, to be able to manage the operation properly. I never intended to work in there. I don't have the expertise.'

Lexi had already noted that Saul was not qualified in chemistry. He did not appear to have enough knowledge to sabotage the protective suits.

'So, when did you last go in?'

'Years ago.'

'And what were you doing on Sunday night, about eight o'clock?'

'Eating.'

'With someone?'

'My family,' Saul replied gruffly.

'Where?'

'At home.'

'Thanks,' Troy said. 'That's all.'

Once the unit director had stomped out of the interview room and slammed the door, Lexi said with a smirk, 'That went well.'

'Mmm. He's south of a rock-solid alibi, isn't he? I'm sure his family will tell us he was at home tucking into Sunday lunch – whether he was or he wasn't.'

'They probably had hot dogs.'

'What did you have?' Troy asked.

'Oven-baked tarantula. And before you say that outers don't have family, I had it with the forensic team while we finished off the last case.'

'I had meatballs with Grandma.'

'And what's in … '

Cutting her off, Troy said, 'They were shiveringly good, so I scoffed the lot. Not a trace left for DNA testing.'

Next, it was the turn of Eric Kiss. Unusually for a major, he had enough of a science background to make the tape that led to the deaths in BSL4.

'Sunday? In the evening?' he muttered. 'I was with Julia.'

'Where?'

'Nowhere in particular. Oh, I see. You're hoping someone saw us who'll provide an alibi. Sorry. Understandably, we keep ourselves to ourselves. We usually make sure we're not seen.'

'That fits. But it's unfortunate,' said Troy. 'For the record, though, where were you?'

'At Julia's place. On our own.'

Later, Julia Nineteen backed up his version of events. 'Almost as if they'd guessed what I'd ask and worked out a good consistent answer,' Troy said with a smile.

Typical of a major, Fern Mountstephen didn't have many qualifications in science but she had worked her way up Shallow End Laboratories, deserving every promotion, meeting every new challenge. According to her records, she was keen and determined.

'You work with a lot of outers,' Troy said to the technician.

'Yes?'

With a grin, he said, 'You must be sick of the sight of them.'

Fern appeared to take his comment seriously. 'As it happens, I don't really notice.'

'Did Blaine do anything odd on Friday?'

'Odd? When?'

'When you did a service on the BSL4 lab.'

She shook her head. 'Not that I noticed.'

'Would you have noticed?'

She shrugged. 'Depends. If he'd broken into a song and a dance, yes, but other things … ' She shuffled in her seat. 'Look. You're alert in the lab, but you tend to concentrate on what's in front of you. You're restricted. Heat builds up. Fatigue sets in. Your eye-shield reflects the lights in the ceiling. It's not easy.'

'If you heard that a major was having a close relationship with an outer, what would you think?'

Fern hesitated. 'Does that happen? It'd be a bit … '

'What?'

'I don't know. Gross maybe.'

'I'm told that's what Brandon Six thought as well.'

'Did he?' Fern was a barrel of a woman. Short, solid and stocky. She gazed at Troy and said, 'If you're hinting about me having relationships with outers, you're right. I do. Good working relationships. And I've got a lot of outer friends. That's all. Anything else would be … ' She shivered.

'I was wondering where you were on Sunday evening. About eight.'

'Er … I was in the local gym. To be precise, I was probably in the swimming pool.'

'Do you get logged in and out again?'

'Yes. You can check if you want.'

'Thanks,' Troy said to end the interview.

The other technician, Blaine Twenty-Two, was highly qualified in chemistry. Troy invited him to sit down and then asked, 'Did Fern do anything odd on Friday?'

'I don't think so.'

Immediately suspicious, Troy said, 'You had a whole day together. You must have done a lot of different things. Don't you want to know which bit I'm interested in?'

'I … er … I assumed you're talking about BSL4, given what happened yesterday.'

'How did you get on with Brandon Six?'

Blaine frowned for a moment. 'What's that got to do with anything?'

'Relationships are always important to an investigation. It's about motives. We tend to kill our enemies, not our friends.'

'You can ask anyone. Brandon was a mate of mine. And, before you ask, I got on fine with Konnie and Tyla as well.'

'Think back to Sunday. What did you do in the evening?'

'Not a lot. I stayed at home and watched television.'

'Can anyone verify that?'

'No.'

'What was on?'

Blaine sneered. 'I drifted a bit but I saw a programme on the build-up to the Integrated Games. The ones where majors and outers compete on equal terms. It's not far from here.'

Troy nodded. 'Okay. That's all for now, thanks.'

The young detectives talked to different members of staff until they had seen everyone on the list – apart from the engineer called Precious Austin. Accessing the company's data files, Lexi said, 'Ah. She was asked to resign a few weeks back. Near the end of last month. When it says "asked", it probably means "forced". Anyway, she couldn't get on with the majority of staff who are outers.'

'Time to put our skates on.'

'What?'

'She's against outers so she's got a motive. No doubt she'll blame them for getting kicked out of her job as well. She's not here so we'll go to her. Is her home address in her file?'

'Yes. On the other side of Shallow End. Second quarter of the main residential zone.'

'Let's go.'

SCENE 9

Tuesday 15th April, Early evening

From the window of Precious Austin's living room, Troy looked out on her garden, with its three neat rows of wooden boxes and a gleaming chrome motorcycle parked by the back fence. Beyond it, there was a field and then the side of the new and impressive sports stadium. Towering over it was a single crane, but the construction job appeared to be complete.

'When the Integrated Games get going, you'll hear

the crowds giving it some welly from here. Good atmosphere,' Troy said.

At once, Precious replied, 'A waste of time and money.'

'Oh? Why's that?'

'Come on!' she retorted. 'Majors and outers competing on a level playing field? That's ridiculous. We'll win the endurance stuff. They'll win the short and fast events. That's not competition. That's genetics. Differences in muscle development and body chemistry.'

'You're an us-and-them person,' said Troy, 'not a we're-all-in-this-together person.'

'Some call us separatists.'

'Us?'

'I can't be the only us-and-them person, as you put it.'

'My grandma would line up with you on that,' Troy said with a smile. He adopted a friendly approach so that Precious would continue to speak freely. 'Is there a separatist organization?'

She scratched her left cheek. 'Not that I'm aware of.'

She was fifty-four years old, according to her file at Shallow End Laboratories. Physically fit, she looked younger than her age. She was slim with long dark hair. Her severe face did not readily form a smile. And Troy was already convinced that she didn't always tell the truth.

'You're an engineer,' he said. 'A job that's more outer than major.'

'If an outer can do it, so can I. It's not like sport, ruled by genes and body make-up.' Precious tapped the side of her head. 'It's about what you've got up here – and determination.'

Fearing that Lexi would butt in with a jibe about the intelligence of majors, Troy said quickly, 'So, let me guess what happened at the labs. They thought you were a bit north of competitive and they asked you to leave.'

'You're very … '

'Perceptive?' Lexi suggested.

Precious avoided looking at Lexi. She made little eye contact with Troy either. 'I was going to say smart.'

'No,' Lexi replied. 'Believe me, he's not smart. He's perceptive.'

Troy forced a laugh. 'She's right. I knew I was perceptive before I was smart enough to know what the word meant.' But Lexi had changed the tone of the interview. It was tense all of a sudden. Troy took advantage and asked Precious, 'Where were you at eight o'clock on Sunday evening?'

'Why? What happened?'

'There was an incident at the laboratories and I'm having to find out where everyone was at the time.'

'But I don't work there any more,' Precious objected.

'But you've got all the know-how you'd need – and, you have to admit, a grievance.'

'I'm out of touch. What happened?' she asked again.

Troy suspected she was already aware of the scientists' deaths. If he was right, she could be feigning ignorance because she was the saboteur. But knowing what had happened didn't necessarily make her guilty. Whilst Troy had not released any information to the media, she could have heard rumblings from members of staff. She could even have talked to someone who worked at Shallow End Laboratories. Still, he played along with her game. 'Calling it an incident will do for now. So, what were you doing on Sunday, eight o'clock in the evening?'

Precious scratched her cheek again. She had engineered plenty of time to think about her answer. Even so, she answered unnaturally slowly. 'I was here. On my own.'

'No one to vouch for you, then?'

'No. But I can guarantee I wasn't up at the labs.'

'Are you sure?' Troy tapped his life-logger. 'You know what you say is being recorded, don't you?'

'Yes, I know. And, yes, I'm sure.'

'Were there any particular outers who complained about you? Ones who ganged up on you and lost you your job?'

'Not really.'

Her body language gave Troy a different answer but she clearly wasn't going to reveal any names. 'Did you work with Brandon Six?'

This time she responded too quickly. 'Yes.'

Knowing that Brandon had disapproved of a relationship that spanned the two human races, Troy asked, 'Did you get on with him okay?'

'There were a lot worse.'

'Such as?'

'Almost all of them.'

Troy wondered if Julia's friendship with Eric Kiss was so repellent to her that it was a motive for murder. 'How about Julia Nineteen?'

'The less said about her,' she growled, 'the better.'

Troy decided to change tactics. 'You must have picked up a lot of science – like chemistry – along the way.'

'I don't have certificates because schools don't expect a major to take an interest. They only encourage outers. I did it the hard way. I taught myself.'

'That's good. I have to rely on Lexi.'

'You don't have to rely on anyone,' Precious retorted. 'You can do it yourself.'

'The thing is,' Troy said, 'I like working in a team.'

For a moment, Lexi took over. 'In the hallway, along with your coats, you've got an all-over suit. What's that for?'

Precious pointed towards the hives in her garden. 'It's obvious, isn't it?'

'Ah. You've swapped a blue suit for a bee suit.'

'I sell honey. And,' she said, 'a bee suit's not so sweaty.'

Troy nodded. 'Okay. That's it for the moment. You're not planning to go away anywhere soon, are you?'

'Why?'

'We might have more questions.'

'I don't know why you should but, no, I don't have travel plans.'

SCENE 10

Tuesday 15th April, Evening

Saul Tingle seemed to be fixed permanently behind his enormous desk. He shuffled uncomfortably in his seat and waved the two detectives towards chairs. 'What can I do for you?'

'We won't keep you long,' Troy said. 'We just need to know who complained about Precious Austin's attitude towards outers.'

Saul sighed. 'No one in particular. It was a general rebellion.'

Troy shook his head. 'Doesn't every mutiny have a ringleader?'

'The final straw was when Tyla Three and Julia came to see me about her.'

'A victim and an intended victim,' Troy pointed out.

'When a laboratory supervisor advises me that animosity could compromise our operations and safety, I have no option but to act.'

'What did you do?'

'I asked Precious to resign.'

'And she did? She didn't put up a fight?'

'I softened the blow with a substantial pay-off,' Saul admitted.

'A golden goodbye,' Troy said with a smile.

'You could call it that.'

'Has she been seen near the building since?'

'Not to the best of my knowledge.'

'And what was her chemistry like? Any good?'

'For a major, remarkable.'

'Thanks,' said Troy, getting to his feet. 'Interesting.'

'Do you think she … ?'

'She ticks some boxes. That's all at this stage.'

'Detective Goodhart,' Saul said. 'You do realize what you're dealing with here, don't you?'

Puzzled, Troy replied, 'I think so.'

There were two drops of moisture on Saul's brow. 'Whoever's got that soil sample, they're a threat to half the world. We could be looking at the extinction of outers.'

'I know.'

'I hope you appreciate the need to resolve it quickly.'

It was Lexi who answered. 'We're not stupid, Mr Tingle. And I'm an outer. If my partner needs reminding about the urgency, I'll take care of it.'

SCENE 11

Tuesday 15th April, Night

Troy watched his grandma's expert hands as she prepared yet another meal. This time it was a kebab. Thinking of Lexi, he asked, 'What's in it, Gran?'

'Loads of salt for flavour and enough fat to keep you going for days.'

'Going where?' he said with a pretend-grimace.

'Troy! You know what I mean.'

'Sorry. What's the meat, though?'

'It's lamb. Sometimes with a bit of beef thrown in. Or chicken. Possibly pork as well, but mainly lamb.'

'Smells good.' While he crushed the blueberries to

make their drinks, Troy said, 'Gran. Have you ever heard of a separatist group? You know. Majors who want separate schooling, separate sport, separate living I suppose. No mixing with outers.'

'It used to be the done thing, honey.'

'Weird.'

'No one kept lions and lambs in the same pen.'

Troy frowned. 'People keep different breeds of dog in the same house. No problem.'

'Nowadays, you young people frown on oldies like me who haven't moved with the times, who don't think all this integration is right.'

Troy washed a little lettuce and cucumber to make the meal healthy. 'But was there an organization that supported separation?'

'Sure, honey. It was called … something.'

'What? Can you remember?'

She put down the long sharp knife and began to push the ill-defined meat into two wallets. 'Apart. That's right. It was something to do with apart. Yes.' She crinkled her face for a moment and then smiled. 'That's it. Two Races Apart. They called it TRAPT for short.'

'Thanks, Gran.'

SCENE 12

Tuesday 15th April, Night

Lexi watched her friends. They were chatting happily, nibbling stir-fried scorpions, drinking, making jokes, poking fun at majors. Not a care in the world. They didn't know that, if her current case went badly, every single one of them could die. She couldn't tell them. Panic wouldn't help. For everyone's sake, she kept the dreadful secret to herself.

If she'd felt able to share the burden, they would have been comforted to hear that she was on the trail of the missing poison, that their future was in her hands. But if she'd told them that their lives also depended on a major, their fear would have been much worse.

'You're quiet tonight, Lexi. Is that new partner bugging you?'

'No.'

'Sure? Something's on your mind.'

'No. He's … okay. Actually, more than okay.'

The others laughed. 'You wouldn't want to trust him with your life, though, would you?'

Lexi hesitated. Even though they didn't know it, all outers were relying on Troy until the sample of SUMP had been found and made safe. That included Lexi. She shrugged. 'I don't get a choice. I have to trust every partner. This one … yeah. If I needed him, I think he'd be there for me.'

'Really?'

'What's more,' she said, 'I reckon he'd be there for you if you needed him.'

Her friend laughed. 'I don't think I'll ever need a major.'

'We'll see.'

SCENE 13

Wednesday 16th April, Early morning

Troy and Lexi looked up at the grand entrance to the sports stadium, the woman labouring up a long ladder with a high-pressure hose in one hand, and the large sign that should have read,

WELCOME TO THE
INTEGRATED GAMES.

Someone had already been up a ladder and sprayed some bright silver paint so that the announcement had become

WELCOME TO THE
DISINTEGRATED GAMES.

'Hey,' Lexi shouted. 'Detective. Don't blast the paint off yet. I need a sample.'

Grumbling, the woman lumbered back down the ladder. She gazed at Lexi and then Troy. 'They're sending detectives now – not one, but two – to catch kids with a spray can and a dodgy sense of humour?'

When Troy and Lexi were racing to save half of humanity, checking out some reported graffiti seemed like overkill and a waste of valuable time, but the defaced sign may not have been the result of a prank. It could have been the work of a violent separatist group.

'Did anyone see who did it?' Troy asked.

'No.'

As Lexi began to climb with a plastic evidence bag and a small knife, Troy explained, 'We're investigating a very serious crime. There's just a chance this is part of it. Have there been any other … incidents aimed at the Integrated Games?'

'No one's died,' she replied drily.

'So, there's been some low-level mischief?'

'You'd have to ask the stadium workers. I'm just a cleaner. But this isn't my first job here. I've cleared up after other bits of vandalism, mischief or whatever you want to call it.'

Troy and Lexi never got the chance to go inside the

sports stadium and talk to the builders. Their life-loggers told them that they were needed urgently by Saul Tingle at Shallow End Laboratories.

SCENE 14

The unit director was almost shaking with fury. 'It arrived in an email at five o'clock this morning,' he said. 'I've set it up in a conference room – on a big screen.'

'One step at a time,' Troy replied. 'What is it?'

'You'll see,' Saul growled. 'It's a video. No sound, just words and pictures.'

Sitting down with the detectives in the conference room, Saul clicked a few keys on his laptop. The screen came alive with a bizarre selection of letters and words in different fonts and sizes, clearly cut-

and-pasted from different sources. There was no voice-over. Somehow, the silence made the caption worse.

*4 MOON suits sabotaged so you **CAN** see how EFFECTIVE **THE** poison is. DID not take **LONG** to **KILL** 3 outers.*

After twenty long seconds, the movie began. It showed three inquisitive white mice, sniffing at the bars of a cage. The camera had clearly been fixed in a position to give a close-up of the cage and a small section of the shelf in front. There was no background in shot. The focus did not change and the footage did not shake. A gloved hand came into the frame. It placed a still-sealed vial in front of the cage.

At once, Troy asked, 'Is that yours? The missing one.'

'Yes. Same type, same label,' Saul answered.

The hand delivered a bowl of water into the cage and another caption appeared.

Water previously **EXPOSED** to **Martian** soil

Within two minutes, the fidgety mice began to slow down. They looked less interested in what was happening. More restless, less curious. One rolled over twice as if drunk. Two of them collapsed at the same time, after another three minutes.

Troy almost whispered, 'Any chance this was filmed here – in one of your secure labs?'

'I don't recognize the type of cage. I'll get someone to check it out.'

'What about the glove?'

Saul shrugged. 'They all look much the same.'

The third mouse lurched, twitched and jumped. It seemed surprised and utterly bewildered by its own movements. Its eyes bulged. Then, frothing at the mouth, it fell over. Before long, it too died.

The short and creepy film ended not with credits but with a final caption.

1 ST DEMAND.
Stop *the* INTEGRATED GAMES.

'First demand,' Troy muttered. 'There'll be others.' He let out a long breath. Turning to Saul Tingle, he asked, 'Could it have been faked?'

'How do you mean?'

'The vial wasn't open. Maybe it was just there for

show. Perhaps SUMP didn't kill the mice. It could have been something else.'

'Like hydrogen cyanide,' Lexi suggested. 'Or some other colourless, poisonous gas.'

Saul shrugged. 'I suppose so. But what are you going to do?'

Lexi said, 'Well, I don't know about you, but I'm pleased to get this.' She waved towards the screen.

Troy nodded. 'You like to get your teeth into a clue.'

'Yeah. Something definite to work on, not just talking to people.'

'I'll send you a copy,' Saul replied. 'But I meant, what are you going to do about the Integrated Games?'

'That's above our heads,' Troy told him. Putting a hand on his life-logger, he said, 'It's already gone to Shepford Crime Central. That's where the decision will come from. Commander McVeigh. But did you notice there wasn't an *or-else* threat?'

'I think it was implied,' Saul said. 'Do what I want or else I'll release the SUMP.'

'That's probably what the powers-that-be will base their decision on.'

'The games will be cancelled, then,' said Lexi.

'Who sent the email?' Troy asked the unit director.

'No one I've heard of. The address was a random selection of letters.'

'As far as you know, are any staff here involved in the games?'

'I don't … Oh. Yes. I remember a conversation. Eric Kiss, Fern Mountstephen and Julia are Friends of the Integrated Games. I think that means they'll be stewards. They volunteered. There might be others.' He shrugged.

'Have you ever heard of an organization called TRAPT?'

'No.'

'Okay. Can you check if the film was made here? It's down to the type of cage, the shelf it was sitting on, and the glove. And that feeding bowl. Are they all Shallow End equipment?'

'I'll see what I can do. Or get hold of someone who can sort it out.' Saul got up and left.

'You might as well forget your bit of silver paint,' Troy said to Lexi.

'Why's that?'

'Because a multiple murderer's in a different league. Whoever's prepared to poison every outer isn't going to risk getting caught by messing around with graffiti.'

'Huh. The motive's obvious now. It's about

keeping the human races apart. If your grandma's right and there's a separatist organization, the spray painter and the poisoner might both be members. One could lead to the other.'

Troy nodded. 'Okay. Good point.'

'First, though,' she said, 'I want to go through this charming little film again. Frame by frame. And I want Terabyte to see if he can work out where it came from.'

SCENE 15

Troy left Lexi to her painstaking examination of the video sequence. At Saul Tingle's suggestion, he went to see Eric Kiss in the animal laboratories instead. Showing him a still from the video on his life-logger, Troy asked, 'Have you got any cages like this?'

Eric examined the image of three mice in a cage and muttered, 'Maybe years ago. They're obsolete now.'

'But have you still got some?'

'I imagine we chucked the lot in a skip but … Follow me. If they're anywhere, they'll be in the old storeroom.' He headed down the corridor towards a fire exit at the back of the building.

On the way, Troy said, 'I heard you volunteered to be a Friend of the Integrated Games. What's that all about?'

Eric grinned. 'I can't run or jump any more – at least, not at competition standard – so I decided to get close to the action as a guide. And, as you know, I like the idea of integration. Julia's joining me, and one or two more, I think.'

Troy chose not to reveal that the future of the Integrated Games was now in doubt.

Eric led him outside, across a courtyard and up to a long and narrow wooden building. He unlocked the door, commenting, 'If the old cages aren't in here, we won't have them any more.'

A passageway running the length of the hut took them past each storage bay. About halfway down the outbuilding, Eric came to an abrupt halt. Pointing to a stack of redundant cages, he said, 'Apparently we do have a few.' He made for the nearest pile.

Troy stopped him with a cry. 'No! This might be part of a crime scene. Don't disturb anything. I think Lexi will want to examine it.' He took a few photographs without approaching the cages. 'Apart from you, who's got a key to get in here?'

'I'm not sure. There's a caretaker. Most of the technicians come in to get things now and again when they're needed in the labs. It's not exactly high security. I suppose the managers have keys as well.'

Troy thrust his life-logger towards Eric and showed him a different still from the video. 'What about that water bowl? Do you have them?'

Eric sighed. 'I think your luck's run out. They're incredibly common. We don't use them now, but everyone with a pet in a cage will have that type.' He carried on down the narrow aisle. 'They'll be here somewhere, I should think.' He found a stack of them near the far end of the shed.

'Last picture,' Troy said, pointing at an image that captured the gloved human hand about to put down the vial. 'Do you recognize the shelf or the glove?'

Eric shook his head. 'Your luck's definitely out. They're just not distinctive enough to say. Sorry.'

SCENE 16

Like all outers, Lexi didn't sleep. She recharged through frequent fifteen-minute periods of meditation. Between studying the digital video and inspecting the outside storeroom, she took a short break to meditate. The case was clearly urgent, but she functioned best if she switched off regularly. She still spent less time out of action than any major, with their need for extended intervals of sleep.

Afterwards, she tucked into a fly burger with gusto. As she ate, she said to Troy, 'The movie's not high quality. Zooming in just gives you blurred pixels. And Terabyte hasn't been able to help with the email. The address came into existence for about five minutes this morning. It was set up in this country, it was used to send the email and then it got wiped. Terabyte noted when the video was recorded, though.'

'Oh?'

'Apparently, in five years' time.' Lexi smiled. 'Which means someone's gone to the trouble of disguising the real timing.'

'What about you?' Troy asked. 'What have you come up with?'

'A few things. It's a left hand that appears, so the person who owns it is either left-handed or pretending to be.'

Almost all outers were left-handed and most majors were right-handed.

Troy said, 'That could be to throw us off the scent – to make us think it's an outer. I imagine our guy's a major.'

'We'll see. The glove's absolutely spotless. Almost certainly new. No stains or wear marks to help me match it with a suspect's glove. So, we've got a careful culprit. I checked the height of the vial and used it as a reference to measure the size of the glove. What can I say? It's not a very reliable method, a small-handed person could have padded it with cotton wool anyway, and the size is medium – like a lot of people's.'

Troy looked at his partner and said, 'I'm waiting for the spark of genius that's uncovered a killer clue.'

'Don't hold your breath,' Lexi replied. 'The feeding bowl hasn't got anything that distinguishes it from any other, but there's a tiny white mark on one of the bars of the cage. The resolution isn't good enough to tell me what it is and it could have been cleaned off by now. In other words, a clever culprit might have put it there on purpose.' Lexi took a deep breath. 'I spent a lot of time on the captions. I wanted to know where the words came from. Most were probably written into a document, printed out from a computer and put on a piece of cardboard, but some of them were cut out from a sports magazine. Or they could be printed out from the online version. Anyway, I guess that's someone's idea of a joke.' She took another bite of the burger made from thousands of compressed flies. She washed it down with cider.

'Taunting us with the sport connection.'

'Yeah. But I think the word "demand" came from an article about a football manager demanding more from his players. It was published yesterday morning. The "effective" probably came from the same source – a boxer developing a more effective left-hand jab.'

Troy nodded. 'Not far off a spark of genius. It tells us the video was shot between yesterday and five this morning when it was emailed to Saul Tingle.'

'There's something else you haven't latched on to.'

'Is there?'

'The cut-out words were put on grey cardboard.' She showed him a close-up on her life-logger. 'See? It's speckled with darker bits. As good as a fingerprint.'

'So,' Troy said, 'we just need to match it … '

'And, hey presto, we've got the film-maker.'

'There's an awful lot of fish in the sea.'

'I thought we were talking cardboard. Anyway, I've sent this picture to manufacturers. If any of them recognize it, they'll let me know. Urgently. That'd narrow it down.'

'Very methodical,' said Troy, with an appreciative grin.

'You follow your feelings. I go with facts.'

'Hey. It's not that simple. I might have instinct but I need you to turn every stone, looking for evidence. If there isn't any … my guts are wrong.'

'Is that where you keep your instinct? Maybe it's right next to those souls you majors say you have.

Obviously I wasn't paying attention in biology lessons.'

Troy tried to keep focused. 'What about the old storeroom?'

'Not good,' she said bluntly. 'Too many people have tramped through it. There are too many shoeprints, fingerprints, fibres and the rest of it. And my life-logger didn't find a matching animal cage. No tell-tale white mark in the right place. Conclusion? The video might have been shot here, and it might not.'

'I hope it was,' Troy replied. 'That'd mean the soil sample's still here, still fairly secure. If it was recorded somewhere else, the poison's out there, closer to being released.'

'Yeah. But would our separatist set it up here and take the risk of someone bursting in while they're filming?'

'Probably less of a risk if it was sometime after midnight. Just the night-shift outers to worry about.'

'I'll set up some spy cameras at all entrances,' Lexi decided. 'And I'm going to have another look at the movie.'

'What for?'

'Shadows and light.' Concentrating on the vial, she said, 'See? No shadow. So, this wasn't shot in sunlight

– which would come in from the side through a window and make a shadow. Assuming there's no window in the ceiling, the room's got an artificial light overhead.'

'You mean like most rooms?'

'Even the smallest thing can help.'

'I hear the sound of a barrel having its bottom scraped.'

'So, what's next, do you reckon?' Lexi asked.

'I don't think we've squeezed all the juice out of Precious Austin yet.'

SCENE 17

With a roll of corrugated cardboard in her left hand, Precious was about to climb into her bee suit when Troy and Lexi called. At once, she abandoned the idea.

Lexi held out her arm and said, 'I'll take a look at the cardboard.'

Precious frowned. 'What? Why?' But she handed it over anyway.

Lexi didn't answer. Instead, she scanned it with her life-logger.

Troy asked, 'What's it for?'

'It's fuel for my smoker.'

'Pardon?'

'You must have seen a bee smoker. It burns things like this type of rolled-up cardboard. It smoulders nicely, making smoke that calms the bees down. Right now, the hives are expanding, almost fully operational. I need to inspect them.' She took the cardboard back from Lexi and said, 'Do outers like you ever eat bees?' The question was almost an accusation.

'Ugh. No. They don't look appetizing at all. We do everyone a favour by stuffing ourselves with maggots, cockroaches, ants and spiders. There are plenty of them and they're usually a nuisance. Flies, grasshoppers and crickets as well.'

Troy sprung an unexpected question on Precious. 'Aren't you a member of TRAPT?'

For an instant, she flinched. 'Of what?'

'TRAPT.'

'TRAPT. I've heard of that. Not recently, though. Wasn't it an old political party or something similar?'

'Look,' Troy said with a weary sigh. 'We're investigating an extremely serious crime that may have been carried out by a member of a separatist organization like TRAPT. If you deliberately refuse to help us, you're putting lives at risk and perverting the course of justice. That carries a prison sentence.'

'I don't know anything about it.'

'I'll do you a deal,' said Troy. 'No names or anything personal. Just tell me when and where the next meeting's happening.'

'You said a deal. What do I get?'

Troy didn't hide his impatience and annoyance. 'It's more what you don't get. You don't get arrested on suspicion of serial killing and perverting the course of justice.'

'If I knew anything ... '

Troy interrupted. 'Why don't you think about it and send the information to me? You can do it anonymously if you like.'

'I'll talk to a few people and see what turns up.'

'Don't linger over it. We're in a hurry.' Before leaving, he asked, 'What did you do with your golden goodbye from Shallow End Laboratories?'

'Golden goodbye? That's a nice way of putting it, but it wasn't very golden. I set myself up with more and better bee-keeping equipment. I'm trying to make a go of my honey-making business.'

SCENE 18

Standing in Commander McVeigh's office at Shepford Crime Central reminded Troy of being back at school. He felt as if he were being quizzed by the head teacher about some misbehaviour. He shuffled from foot to foot. Beside him, Lexi did not seem so edgy. She was usually more relaxed than Troy.

'The Integrated Games will be cancelled, of course,' the chief of police told them. 'The media office is preparing to release the news. But there'll be no mention of the real reason. There'll be a safety issue – a flaw in the stadium structure – because we must avoid alarm at all costs. The investigation will be conducted very sensitively. Do you understand me?'

Troy and Lexi both nodded.

The commander looked at them in turn. 'It's the most important case ever on my patch and I'm aware that you're inexperienced. Are you confident that you can bring it to a satisfactory conclusion – or would you prefer to surrender it?'

The young detectives glanced at each other. At once, Troy read Lexi's mood from her expression. 'We haven't hit the buffers yet. We're making progress and we want to stick with it.'

'You're top of Crime Central's priorities. Anything you want – backup, more forensics, anything at all – you'll get immediately.'

'Thank you, but we're okay at the moment.'

'Good. Because a tight team keeps information contained,' Commander Cheryl McVeigh said. 'The fewer people who know what's happening, the better. The less leaks out. But if you call for more officers, you'll get them. They'll crack on with whatever you want them to do, but we'll avoid giving them the whole picture.'

Troy and Lexi nodded their agreement.

McVeigh added, 'Remember, there's no shame in asking a more seasoned detective to step in.'

Lexi's life-logger began to vibrate.

'If it's to do with the case,' the commander said, 'take it.'

Lexi read the message. 'It's the cardboard used in the video. I've got its source.'

'Good. But before I let you get on with it, I need to ask you both the same question. For the sake of half of the human races, you must give me an honest answer. First, Troy. Do you believe your current partner is the best person for this job?'

Without turning towards Lexi, Troy said, 'Yes. I can't imagine anyone better.'

'Lexi Four. You're the more experienced detective in this team. You've had a few different partners and you've been outspoken and critical of their merits. You're also an outer so your life is on the line here. Think carefully. Is Detective Goodhart the best person to help you complete this assignment?'

Lexi glanced sideways before answering, 'Yes. He's ... '

'What?' she asked.

'Perceptive.'

'Perceptive? That's what his record says. And very little else.'

'He's thorough as well. Probably better than all my previous partners. Mind you, they were ... '

'This isn't a time for joking.'

'It wasn't a joke. It was going to be an honest assessment of previous majors.'

'Enough. You're both satisfied with the current arrangement. For now, I'm prepared to leave you in charge of the case – but only on the understanding that you'll request a more experienced officer on the slightest suspicion that you need assistance or advice. Are we all on the same wavelength?'

At the same time, Troy and Lexi answered, 'Yes.'

'Now, do you want to ask me anything else?'

Troy knew that his superior was hinting. 'About what?' he prompted.

'I listened to the interview you've just had with Precious Austin. Not surprisingly, you got frustrated.'

Troy realized what was on the chief's mind. 'She knows something about a separatist group called Two Races Apart. TRAPT. Do you know anything about it?'

Glancing at Lexi, Commander McVeigh said, 'You're right. He's perceptive.' Addressing Troy again, she said, 'No, not really. But I know a man who does. An undercover officer. Dominic Varney. He infiltrated TRAPT a while ago, but I don't recall any important feedback so we sent him to prison instead. Kindale Prison. Not an enviable place to be. He unearthed a lot of intelligence there. He's out now. Undercover work takes its toll, though. Sometimes, you get too bound up with the organization you're supposed to be investigating. You play the bad boy's role so well that you become a bad boy. So, I've given him a period of leave – to readjust. When he was undercover, he wasn't wearing a life-logger, of course, so there's no official record. It's all word of mouth. But maybe he can throw some light on TRAPT for you.'

'Thanks.'

'I've been in contact and he's going to meet you in Cloverleaf Park at seven thirty.'

'Okay. That's good.'

'Dismissed. And good luck.'

Striding along the corridor, Troy was the first to speak. 'Thanks for what you said in there.'

'Huh. Ditto.'

'Tell me about cardboard.'

'It's fascinating stuff.'

Troy frowned. 'Is it?'

'No. A company recognized it as theirs, though. It's a cheap recycled product. No great strength but they sell it for packaging – wrapping plates, ornaments and that sort of thing.'

'Do makers of scientific glassware wrap their vials and other bits and pieces in it before they're shipped out to places like Shallow End Laboratories?'

Lexi smiled. 'That's what I'm going to check when we're back there.'

SCENE 19

Wednesday 16th April, Early evening

A cool breeze blew around Cloverleaf Park as daylight began to fade, but there was no rain. Troy and Lexi sat on one of the benches. Lexi watched the lights of Shepford turning on one at a time, like stars coming into view at nightfall. Troy glanced anxiously around the park. It wasn't huge; roughly circular with a perimeter path. From where they were sitting, Troy could turn his head and see almost every metre of the track. At seven thirty-two, he was relieved to see a well-built middle-aged man in shorts and T-shirt enter from the gate to the right and run towards them.

He didn't stop, though. He glanced at them as he jogged past. That's all. No acknowledgement, no smile, no greeting. He continued his run around the perimeter.

'That'll be him,' Troy said to his partner. 'He's cautious. Checking the area out first.'

'We'll see.'

Five minutes later, having completed one lap, the runner came to a halt nearby, dropped onto the dry grass and began exercising with some press-ups. 'Goodhart and Lexi Four, presumably.'

'Yes.' Troy opted for a casual approach. 'Enjoying your freedom?'

'Yeah, man. The only good thing to say about doing time is that I got in shape. Not much to do but work out in the prison gym. Apart from that, Kindale was the pits.' The major detective stifled an ironic laugh. 'I reckon the governor spent more on feeding his dogs than the inmates. And when the dogs were sick, they got a visit from the vet straightaway. Prisoners didn't get to see doctors or medicine unless they were halfway to the crematorium.' He switched to squat thrusts. 'And the cockroaches! They crawl all over you at night. I went to bed in gloves to stop them chewing my fingernails while I was asleep. But they still get inside your ears to eat the wax. Sometimes, you'd swallow one. You can feel it moving around in your stomach.'

'Mmm. Nice,' Lexi said.

Dominic Varney smiled grimly. 'No need to ask who's the outer.' For a moment, he stopped exercising and took some deep breaths. 'I like this park. No security cameras.'

'TRAPT,' Troy prompted.

'Ah, yes. The boss said you'd want to know.' He stood up and began a series of star jumps. On each jump, he rotated so he could survey the whole of the darkening park furtively. 'Not many members, not well organized, weren't planning anything illegal. No one planning a massacre. Basically a small, sad bunch of losers and bigots. Best to leave them alone, man.'

Troy walked across the track, onto the grass, and held up his life-logger showing a picture of Precious Austin. 'Was she one of them?'

'Yes.'

'How about … ?' He pressed keys until he got an image of Fern Mountstephen.

Dominic shook his head. 'Never seen her.'

'And this one?'

Dominic didn't recognize Eric Kiss either. He also drew a blank with Brandon Kane Six. But he hesitated over a picture of Saul Tingle. 'Er … no. Not at TRAPT anyway.'

'Have you come across him somewhere else?'

'Um. He looks vaguely … No. He's like someone else. That's all.'

'Were there any outers in TRAPT?'

'I'll answer that,' Dominic said, 'in four and a half minutes.' Then he took off along the path.

When Troy sat down next to Lexi again, she said, 'I guess you have to be bonkers to do undercover work.'

'Mmm. You also have to be an expert at deceiving people.'

Lexi frowned. 'Do you think he's lying or something?'

'I'm not sure. He's hard to read. That's what makes him good at his job.'

'What's bothering you?'

'He said, "No one's planning a massacre." Almost as if he knows about the missing SUMP. But Cheryl McVeigh wouldn't have told him. She wants it under wraps. Too many cooks spoil the sausage.'

Lexi shrugged. 'Perhaps it was just a jokey comment – and a coincidence.'

'He would've become a militant separatist to infiltrate TRAPT. I just hope he hasn't stayed that way.'

A detective often had to think the same way as a

crook. Both moved in the margins of society. Especially an undercover officer. But something would have gone horribly wrong if a detective and a criminal had become indistinguishable. The thought brought back unwelcome memories and made Troy shudder.

Only slightly out of breath, Dominic went back down to ground in front of the bench and began more press-ups. He carried on talking as if there hadn't been an interruption. 'I didn't take a DNA testing kit – or ask to see their fingertips – but I doubt it. They didn't think kindly of outers.'

'Can you give me all the names you remember?'

Dominic chuckled. 'Here's the thing. They never used real names. They gave themselves nicknames. I think it made them feel important and secretive. Like spies.'

'What was your nickname?'

'Mine?' For a moment, the undercover officer seemed taken aback by an unexpected question. 'Gritty – because of my stamina.'

'No doubt, it helps to be gritty in your line of work. You must have to learn a whole heap of stuff for every assignment.'

'That's right.'

'Have you ever had a job in science?' Troy asked.

'About a year ago. A pharmaceutical company that was shipping some illegal pills.'

'Did you have to get to grips with chemistry?'

'Yes. A nightmare. Not the most exciting topic.'

Troy laughed. 'I'm with you on that. But sorry, I've strayed. Back to TRAPT. Where do they meet?'

'The community centre in Shepford's second quarter. The one dominated by majors. It was always booked under a variety of names. Never TRAPT, of course. Sometimes it was the Shepford Political Debating Society. Not a name that got people queuing at the door.'

'And you definitely didn't come across anyone thinking about atrocities against outers?'

'No.'

'Not even someone saying, "I could murder the lot of them," as a sort of joke?'

'Not that I heard.'

'Okay. Thanks for your help. Enjoy the rest of your holiday.'

As soon as Dominic pounded towards the park exit, Troy murmured, 'Slippery customer.'

Troy wasn't sure if Dominic Varney was a hero or a villain. Had he sacrificed a normal life for the public good? Had he ventured so far undercover that he was no longer a functioning police officer? Had he gone rogue?

'He made the TRAPT people sound harmless,' said Lexi.

'Yes. Like little angels with strange ideas.'

'Are real people like that? Me, I've threatened to throttle every major.'

Troy nodded as they got up and trudged back to the car. 'When they're having a strop, young majors say they could murder their parents, brother or sister. Everyone lets off steam now and again. That's another reason I don't know what to make of him.'

SCENE 20

The journey from the park to Shallow End Laboratories took fifteen minutes. The perfect time for Lexi to refresh her mind by turning off and meditating. Troy stared out of the window and wondered. Later, he would sleep while Lexi kept going.

In the technical supplies department, Lexi picked up some cardboard packaging and said, 'Does a lot of your glassware arrive wrapped in this?'

'Not all of it, but quite a bit, yes.'

Scanning the speckled card with her life-logger and using pattern recognition software, Lexi came up with a ninety per cent match with the roll that Precious Austin used in her smoker and the background for the words in the video.

'You must have an awful lot to get rid of. What happens to it?'

'We leave it out for recycling – in the big bin at the back – but the staff who've got a use for it take it home.' He shrugged. 'Re-using is better than recycling.'

'Who takes it?' Lexi asked.

The technician shrugged again. 'I'm just pleased to see the pile's smaller in the morning.'

'Have you seen Precious Austin recently?'

'Not for a while, no. But, now you mention it, she used to take quite a lot. Building up a stock of it for some reason.'

SCENE 21

Back at Crime Central, Lexi said, 'Okay. Time to pull together all the information we've got into a spreadsheet. I can tidy it up overnight while you're dreaming about sausages or whatever.'

Troy smiled. 'You get itchy without an orderly gathering of the facts.'

'I get itchy when someone's threatening every outer with imminent death. So, let's lay it all out properly. That way, I can see where we are much more clearly. And I've got all the facts at my fingertips.'

Outers did not have fingerprints so Troy could not

resist saying, 'No jokes about you not having anything else at your fingertips.'

'Huh. No one knows why majors have got fingerprints anyway. They don't have a purpose – apart from giving you away at crime scenes. Come on,' she said. 'Motive first.'

'Easy. It's about keeping the human races apart.'

'More than that,' Lexi replied. 'It's about genocide with an unstoppable poison from Mars. For some strange reason, nature's decided to let all you majors off. Your body's evolved so it's not affected.'

'As far as we know.'

'Yeah, okay. But it's certain ours would take a hit. Nature got the design wrong.'

'Both are brilliant designs really.'

'Are they?'

'The body's a miracle of engineering. And … '

'Go on.'

'Miracles are what God does,' said Troy.

'That's the nonsense I thought you were heading for. But how many people do you know with bad backs? Then there's giving birth. Ask any major mother what she thinks of the way it's done. And us outers can't do it at all any more. Not naturally anyway. Is that really a miracle?'

'An imperfect miracle, but still a miracle. Look at

the human brain. It's amazing what it can do. It can even come up with spreadsheets. No other animal makes spreadsheets.'

'You're stopping me making one as well. Come on. Suspects. The obvious ones are all majors. Agreed?'

'Yes.'

'Right. Name. Do they have the motive? Do they know enough about science? Do they have access to the BSL4 lab? Alibi for Sunday evening. That's five columns. I'll start with Precious Austin. She's got enough of a grievance against outers and she's a separatist. She's probably got enough knowledge of science. She's not on the Shallow End site any more but could have sneaked into it and she's trained to go into containment level four. No Sunday evening alibi. Surely she's our number one.'

Troy nodded. 'There's something we need to find out. When did she leave the labs? Did she work on SUMP or even know about it? Because our bad guy certainly does.'

'Next is Saul Tingle,' Lexi continued. 'No known motive, probably not enough of a background in science, but he could go into the high-security lab and his alibi for Sunday evening isn't strong. Eating with his family.'

'What about Fern Mountstephen?' said Troy.

'Yeah. She doesn't like outers and majors to get as close as Julia Nineteen and Eric Kiss.'

'But she's a Friend to the Integrated Games. Or was, when they were still on. That suggests she approves of mixing.'

'Yeah. And she sounded … comfortable with outers. She talked about having outer friends. So,' Lexi said, 'not much of a motive. But she's probably up enough in science to make the sticky tape. And she's a regular at handling poisons in BSL4.'

'A solid alibi for Sunday, though,' Troy reminded her. 'I checked with her gym. She was there all evening.'

Lexi sighed. 'Eric Kiss. He distracted the lab supervisor at the time of the deaths.'

'But where's his motive? He seems to like outers – or at least one outer. He wouldn't try to kill Julia Nineteen.'

'If he's not faking it with her. Anyway, he's got the scientific know-how and access to the lab, and his Sunday evening alibi is weak. He was hiding out with Julia.'

'I want Dominic Varney on the list.'

'Really? A serving police officer?'

'Yes. Not our top suspect, but he researched chemistry and worked in a pharmaceutical lab. He's been exposed to separatists and maybe he got radicalized.'

'You didn't ask him what he was doing on Sunday evening.'

'I didn't want to ruffle his feathers. I needed him to think he was a witness, not a suspect.'

'Okay. Sunday evening alibi – unknown. What about access to Shallow End's lab?'

'Mmm. That's another unknown.'

'Anyone else? Anything else?'

'Not yet.'

'Okay. I'll write it up and work on the paint sample – and anything else I can think of. You go and rest your poor exhausted major body.'

SCENE 22

Lexi liked working through the night. At night Crime Central wasn't cluttered with majors. Almost everyone was an outer. Most of the scientists were conducting forensic tests. A few were meditating in quiet rooms and quiet corners. No one interrupted the cleansing of their minds. No one made jokes about sleeping on the job. Lexi's fondness for the night-time shift didn't make her a separatist. She liked being with her own kind, but she also valued the input of majors – at least from the ones that were good at what they did. Sometimes, she felt, a job would be given to a major to keep the numbers equal when an outer would have been a far better choice.

She peered down the microscope at a few of the shiny flecks of paint from the graffiti at the sports stadium and took a few close-up shots. At first sight, the shavings looked similar to a lot of glossy silver paints, but she knew that the light reflecting from each type gave a distinctive range of wavelengths. She used microspectrophotometry to record the signature colours.

Revealing the chemical composition of the paint would tell her more. She prepared a piece for X-ray analysis. Afterwards, she burnt a few of the fragments and analysed the gases by chromatography to identify the resin and pigments. She finished her examination with infrared spectroscopy to confirm the organic constituents.

Then, armed with the exact colour and the chemical components of the paint, she began a search through databases to see if she had enough information to find its manufacturer. She also sent her results to the Paint Research Department to see if specialists could provide any extra help.

After her second meditation of the night, with her mind especially sharp, she pinpointed the source of the silver paint. Her data matched a specialized product designed to give a mirror-like chrome effect to almost any surface. It was used mostly by motorcycle enthusiasts. Shortly after her conclusion, an expert at the Paint Research Department contacted her with the same result.

Most road vehicles had become driverless years ago. But not motorcycles. They'd kept their reputation as the ideal way for free spirits to travel. Motorcyclists still weaved in and out of traffic, speeding along congested roads, tackling tracks too rough or narrow for cars. Somewhere out there was a free spirit that Lexi and Troy would like to interview.

Lexi also requested a trace on Dominic Varney's phone. It didn't take long. The mobile had been stationary at his house on Sunday evening.

She looked up details on the pharmaceutical company that Dominic had infiltrated last year. It specialized in drug treatments for infectious diseases. And at once, Lexi drew in a breath. She searched the company's website for details of its facilities. She smiled when she found what she wanted. To develop cures for contagious bacteria and viruses, their researchers had BSL3 and BSL4 laboratories.

Lexi sat back. Maybe her partner was onto something. Undercover, Dominic Varney may well have learned the skills needed to work in a high-security laboratory.

Bringing up her spreadsheet on her monitor, she altered Dominic Varney's entries. Tracking his mobile phone had not provided him with a strong alibi for Sunday and his undercover work may well have set him up to enter the Shallow End site and gain access to the crime scene.

She sent her results to Troy Goodhart's life-logger.

SCENE 23

As soon as Troy saw Lexi's overnight results, even before breakfast, he arranged to meet her outside Precious Austin's house. 'To catch a worm,' he said on the phone, 'you've got to be an early bird. Bring your evidence bags and something to scrape paint.'

Waiting for his partner by the front garden, Troy watched bees investigating the wallflowers and primroses. When Lexi arrived, she asked, 'What's on your mind?'

'Didn't you see what Precious had at the bottom of her back garden?'

'No.'

'A motorbike – with plenty of chrome.'

Lexi smiled. 'I've always fancied riding one. I like the way they take corners. I'd like to feel that sort of speed with one knee centimetres from the road surface.'

'Just scrape the paintwork, not your knee.'

Precious Austin was not pleased to see the two detectives again, but she didn't seem surprised. 'Yes,' she admitted, 'I use a chrome-type spray paint. I like to keep the bike looking good. Why?'

Ignoring her question, Troy asked, 'Have you still got the spray can?'

'No. Do you want to go into my workshop to prove it?'

'No. Lexi will just take a sample off the bike.'

'What?' She looked horrified.

'A tiny scrape will do. No one'll notice.'

Precious glanced at Lexi. 'Do you have to?'

'No. I could take a great big bit instead. A scratch that everyone'll see.'

Precious scowled at her. 'You know what I mean. Are you being deliberately provocative?'

Troy smiled to himself. His partner *was* being deliberately provocative. She wouldn't admit it, though. But it was what Precious deserved.

Lexi said, 'I'll take as much as I need – which isn't very much.'

While Lexi went for the sample and Precious eyed her carefully from the window, Troy asked, 'When did you leave the Shallow End job?'

'Three weeks ago. Friday the twenty-first of March.'

'Are you going to tell me when the members of Two Races Apart are getting together?'

'I've got no idea.'

'But you're a member. I've got a witness who says so.'

'Are you sure?'

'A reliable witness. There's no doubt.'

'In that case, yes, it's tonight at eight thirty.'

'The community centre in the second quarter? Not far from here?'

'So I've been told,' she replied.

Afterwards, Troy looked at the small evidence bag in his partner's hand and its streak of silver paint. 'If it matches, it's yet another piece of evidence against her. But does it make her look more guilty – or more innocent?'

'Innocent?'

'Exactly.'

'How do you make that out?'

Troy explained, 'I still can't believe that someone

splattering graffiti on a sports stadium is the same person who's threatening an outer massacre. They're worlds apart. Would a murderer spray evidence against themselves over a public wall? It just doesn't figure.'

'All I do is get evidence,' Lexi said, 'but, if you want me to tread in your territory, what about a double bluff?'

Troy frowned. 'You mean, she wanted us to pin the graffiti on her because we wouldn't believe that the vandal and the murderer were the same person?'

'Result? We dismiss her as a murder suspect.'

Troy sighed. 'Well, she left her bike out where we'd see it, but even so … I'm not buying it. Something's telling me … '

'What?'

'It's just too easy. She's not a fool. Would someone so clever make it so easy?'

'Don't ask me. You're the one who's good on human behaviour. I just think if she's that clever, she could work out a double bluff.'

SCENE 24

Thursday 17th April, Morning

Lexi worked on the paint sample while she nibbled at her breakfast, laid out in front of her like an entomologist's display. Troy concentrated solely on his black pudding and curry sauce. By the time he'd finished, Lexi announced, 'Hey presto. It matches. That's not proof Precious Austin's our graffiti artist, but it's not bad. Do you want to arrest her on suspicion of defacing a public building?'

'Not really,' Troy replied, wiping his mouth. 'I want to catch a multiple murderer who's holding every outer on the planet to ransom.'

'And I haven't convinced you they're the same person?'

'No.' Troy paused before asking, 'Do you want to arrest her?'

'No. If she's playing a double bluff game, I don't want her to think it's working. It'd be better to keep her in the dark about what we're doing.'

'Agreed.'

'By the way,' Lexi added, 'last night I went through footage from my spy cameras outside Shallow End Laboratories. Nothing.'

'I think the horse has already bolted.'

The giant water beetle on Lexi's plate was about seven centimetres long. It had been lightly boiled and salted. She picked it up and said, 'Saved the best till last.' First, she yanked off and threw away the tough and inedible wings. Next, she detached the head. Some juice oozed out as she squeezed and pulled. A few sticky strings of saliva stretched out like melted cheese as the head came off. Then she tucked into the body, sucking all of the meat out of it. 'It's a bit like prawn,' she told Troy. 'And liquorice.' She put down the empty shell and said, 'Now for the highlight. The head. This one's too strong to bite through, so … ' She used her finger to extract the lump of meat from inside and popped it into her mouth. 'Mmm. Like crab and liquorice.'

Troy grimaced. 'It's more like watching a biology practical than breakfast.'

Lexi smiled. 'You eat prawns and lobster, don't you? You rip them apart to get to the meat.'

'Not if meatballs are on offer instead,' Troy replied. He looked down at his life-logger and immediately the mood changed. 'We've got another demand. Just a photo this time.'

'Yeah.' Lexi was looking at it on her own life-logger.

The image contained the familiar vial and cardboard background. Only the words were different.

2nd demand.
We eat DIFFERENT *things.*
We **must** *have* separate *eating* PLACES.

Lexi shook her head and sighed. 'First, the sports stadium. Now, restaurants. What next? Schools? Whole towns?'

Thinking of one of his favourite mixed restaurants, Troy muttered, 'No way. I love The Hungry Human.'

'This is a point of principle,' Lexi said. 'It's about apartheid. Not just a threat to a diner you happen to like.' She transferred the image to her computer and displayed it on the large screen.

'I was using The Hungry Human as a way of life. A place to mix. The opposite of apartheid.' Attempting a grin, Troy added, 'And they cook a mean sausage.'

'The message went to Saul Tingle – like the last one – and he forwarded it to us,' Lexi said. 'And it's cut-out words again – from magazines or printed out from online articles.'

'They came from sporting pieces last time,' Troy replied. 'Just to rub it in. So, let's check if these are from restaurant reviews, recipes, and that sort of thing.'

Lexi nodded. 'Yeah. We'll see. Good thinking.' She hesitated, peering at the magnified image, and then said, 'Actually, you do it while I go over this picture.'

'I can do better than one pair of eyes. I'll ask the commander to put fifty of her best people onto it. That'll speed it up.'

They worked quietly and separately until Troy said, 'I've just been told someone's identified the word *DIFFERENT*. Looks like it comes from a magazine advert for a restaurant. "Fancy tasting something different?" The font, colour and size are identical. I'm sending you the source. That's source with an "o", not sauce with everything.'

'Huh.'

'How are you getting on with the picture? Found anything?'

'Yes,' Lexi said. 'Give me a couple of minutes to do the maths and I'll show you.'

Almost exactly two minutes later, Lexi pointed at a spot at the bottom of the card, near the centre. 'See that?'

Troy saw very little. 'There's a slight mark. A shadow?'

Lexi smiled. 'I've enhanced it. This is what it looks like after I let loose the best software for defining shape – the sort of thing they use to map craters on the moon.' She tapped the screen to bring up a detail of the area. 'I found a crater in the cardboard.'

The image wasn't entirely clear but there was definitely a small, round dent. 'It's got a ridge around the edge, hasn't it?' Troy asked. 'And a line – not quite vertical – in the middle. Weird.'

'I'm sure it's the impression of a button. The card's corrugated, so it's soft, and I think someone wearing a long-sleeved shirt or blouse has leant on the card when they arranged the message. If the sleeve had a cuff, pressing down would leave a dent in the shape of the button. That's what we've got. The line's the thread between the holes, I think.'

'Fantastic. Can you measure its size?'

'Not directly,' Lexi replied. 'But I measured the height of the letters of DIFFERENT from a life-size version of the online food magazine. That gives me a scale to work to. If I use the same ratio on the impression of the button, hey presto, it's got a diameter of twelve millimetres. Plus or minus half a millimetre.'

'Great. We're looking for someone wearing a sleeve with a cuff held together by a twelve-millimetre button.'

'Not a four-hole one. It's a two-hole button because the thread's just a line.'

'Nice work,' Troy said, nodding at his partner. 'It's a little needle in a big haystack, but it's a lot better than nothing.'

'Yeah.'

Troy pointed to the left of the impression. 'Is that orange mark part of the cardboard?'

'I'm not sure, but I don't think so. It's like a grain of sand. But I can't do much with a photo. If I had the actual thing in front of me, I'd be able to tell you. There's another orangey brown splodge near the top as well.' She shrugged, frustrated by the lack of physical evidence.

Remembering that they needed to find out if Precious Austin worked on SUMP or knew about its toxicity, Troy called Julia Neve Nineteen at Shallow End Laboratories and asked, 'When exactly did you get the Mars soil sample? And when did you start working on it?'

'The beginning of March.'

'What date?'

Julia was silent for a while, obviously checking her records. 'Tuesday the fourth.'

'And did you start working on it straightaway?'

'Almost. Once we'd housed it safely and split the sample between the three different cupboards, we began testing on the Wednesday.'

'Did Precious Austin get involved?'

'No. She was on a different line of research.'

'Did you discover how lethal it was before she left on the twenty-first?'

'Mmm. Let me … ' There was a gap of about fifteen seconds before the lab supervisor replied. 'Yes. We knew it killed outer cells by then. My notes on the eighteenth say we suspect there's a Martian microorganism that incapacitates outers' metabolism but doesn't affect the cell chemistry of majors.'

'So, Precious might well have known that result before she lost her job?'

'I suppose so.'

'Thanks.'

Lexi listened to her partner's conversation while she checked if she'd received any more messages. When Troy finished the call, she said, 'Last night, I sent a request for information on what Dominic Varney had learned at the pharmaceutical lab he'd infiltrated.'

'Didn't he use an alias?'

'Yes. I got that from the commander's office first. The important thing is,' she said, nodding towards her life-logger, 'they've just told me he worked in all containment levels. Including four.'

Troy raised his eyebrows. 'Time to go and take a look at his shirtsleeves?'

SCENE 25

Lexi and Troy discovered Dominic Varney in his front garden. The undercover police officer turned to face Troy with a chainsaw in his hand. Just for an instant, Troy spotted annoyance in his face. When the fleeting expression vanished, Dominic nodded towards the nearest tree. 'It's an ash and it's got a fungal disease. It's coming down.'

'That's harsh,' Troy replied.

Dominic shook his head. 'When there's an infection going round, killing off a whole species, it's best to be ruthless. Chopping down and burning reduces the risk of it spreading.'

Troy wondered whether his attitude would be the same if a bacterium from a Martian soil sample were to infect and kill outers. 'I've got to ask you what you were doing at eight o'clock on Sunday evening.'

Dominic scowled at him and then carefully put down the chainsaw at the base of the doomed tree. 'I can't tell you that, man.'

'Why not?'

'What's made me move from witness to suspect?'

'Hopefully just a few coincidences. You can move back again easily enough. Just tell me about Sunday night.'

'No can do.'

'Where were you, then? I'd be satisfied if you can prove you were well away from our crime scene, even if you won't tell us what you were up to.'

'No can do,' he repeated.

The cuffs of his shirtsleeves were protruding from the arms of his jacket. While he was talking to Troy, Lexi took a sneaky photograph of the nearer cuff.

'So, there's something more important than getting off our list of suspects?'

'Spot on.'

'Okay. You know how it works. I've got to put you down as not having an alibi, meaning we'll have to poke around some more.' Troy didn't hesitate. 'Lexi's going to want to take a photo of every shirt you've got.'

'You've got a clue, then. Some material? A make? A size?'

'Does she have your permission to go inside and crack on?'

Dominic shrugged. 'Be my guest. You'll find them in the upstairs wardrobe. And maybe a couple in the washing basket. That's the lot.'

While Lexi went inside, Troy asked, 'How did you find working in a high-security lab?'

Realizing that Troy and Lexi had been researching his recent past, Dominic grinned. 'Those overalls are seriously unpleasant, man. Before you know it, you fill the gloves with sweat.'

'Yuck.'

'Made me feel like a goldfish, looking out of a bowl.'

Troy wanted to know if Dominic still had access to a chemistry laboratory, but he didn't ask because it was pointless. If the undercover officer was guilty, he'd deny making hi-tech sticky tape that could ooze acid. He'd deny storing a sample of alien soil too. So, his answers would be the same as an innocent person's. Troy hoped that Lexi would quickly look for any locked or hidden rooms that could house a secret laboratory.

'What did Commander McVeigh tell you about what we're investigating?'

'Very little. A serious hate crime. And that my knowledge of TRAPT might help your enquiries. That's all. It doesn't take much to work out that you're looking into a major versus outer quarrel. Then, yesterday, you asked me about anyone – a major, I assume – plotting atrocities against outers. Now you're going on about lab protection suits, I'm guessing it's got something to do with science as well.' He shrugged. 'I'm on holiday. I don't want to know any more.'

Probing Dominic's opinion of outers would also be pointless. He would not admit to prejudice even if he loathed the whole species. Instead, Troy said, 'When you're undercover, you must mix with a lot of dodgy characters. You must be expert at hiding your real feelings about them.'

'It goes with the territory. Why? Do you think I'm hiding a deep-seated hatred of outers?'

'My point is, I wouldn't know. But I'll try to find out.'

'And how do you propose to do that?'

Troy shrugged. 'I could look at your record of arrests. I'd guess it'd be about a fifty-fifty mix of majors and outers. If there were a lot more outers, that might suggest something.'

Dominic looked unconcerned. 'I wouldn't have a clue what my ratio is. That's how little it means to me, man. I acted like a bigot in TRAPT, but I'm not one. I'm not your bad guy.'

Troy smiled. 'You're a good actor, though.'

He nodded. 'I'll admit to that.' He bent down to pick up the chainsaw again. 'But telling the difference between truth and lies is your problem, not mine.'

'I'll go in and see how Lexi's getting on.'

Dominic was either comfortable with his innocence or completely confident that his guilt was well concealed. Carefree, he replied, 'Okay.'

Troy made for the door while, behind him, came the loud growl of the chainsaw, hungry for timber.

Troy found Lexi peering slyly inside a ground-floor study. 'Is that where he keeps his shirts?' Troy asked with a grin.

'I've done all that,' she told her partner in a whisper. 'I was just wondering if he's converted a room into a lab. Nothing so far. I can't be too long or he'll get suspicious. But I'd like to check an outbuilding at the back.'

'He's busy. Listen,' said Troy. 'That's his chainsaw. We'll be okay while he's making that noise.'

Unseen, the saw's motor idled for a few seconds and then revved into action once more.

Together, Troy and Lexi crept out of the back door and into the rear garden. They crossed the lawn towards a wooden structure. It was too large and solid to call a shed, but not large and solid enough to be a cottage. They were half way across the grass when the chainsaw fell silent.

Caught in no man's land, they decided to carry on. But, when they were five metres from the door, Dominic's voice called out, 'No shirts in there.'

They turned towards the detective. He was standing at the corner of the lawn with the saw still in his hand.

Troy didn't try to disguise the fact that they were having a sneaky inspection of his home. 'What is in it?'

Dominic lifted the chainsaw to waist height. 'I take my gardening seriously. Tools. You can't go in right now because it's locked. No key on me.'

'Never mind,' Troy said. 'Lexi's finished anyway. We're off.'

'Good,' Dominic replied.

In the car, Troy muttered, 'Strange he didn't have a key for his shed. How did he get the chainsaw out?'

'As far as I could see, if he's got a chemistry lab, it'll be in his hut.'

Troy nodded. 'We may have to go back but, for now, how did you get on?'

Lexi tapped some keys on her life-logger. 'He's got one shirt with a button that could've made the impression. It falls within the error limits.'

'I feel a "but" coming on.'

'If it was the only button in the world that fits … Hey presto, we've got our man. But we don't know how common it is.'

'So it's good evidence but south of definite. It keeps him on the hit list.'

'Yeah.'

'I've been checking out his record of arrests.' Troy glanced at his own life-logger. 'He's bagged far more outers than majors. And that's not all.'

'Oh?'

'There are some bits of kit that aren't accounted for.'

'Such as?'

'He had some miniature surveillance stuff and he hasn't returned it yet. Like a spy camera.'

·'What else?'

'A couple of bugs.'

'For listening or eating?' Lexi asked with a smile.

SCENE 26

The Hungry Human was not a happy place. The waiter complained, 'All of a sudden, the powers-that-be are coming down on mixed menus like a ton of bricks. I don't know why. It doesn't make sense. They seem to want us to cater for outers or majors but not both. That's not what we're about.'

Lexi nodded. 'So you're still going to serve us? An outer and a major?'

'Of course. It's what we do.'

'Good for you,' Troy replied.

They each ordered a lunch. While they waited, Troy whispered, 'I want to gate-crash the TRAPT meeting tonight but I can't. Precious Austin might have warned them about me. She might even be there to point me out. We can't send Dominic Varney in. He's a pro at undercover work and he's been before, but he's looking more and more like a serious suspect. Sadly. And you can't go because you're an undesirable – an outer.'

'There's an obvious solution.'

'What's that?'

'You go in disguise.'

'Tell me you're joking.'

'Okay,' Lexi said quietly. 'I'm joking. But … '

'No.'

'You'd look good as … '

'No. I'm not clutching at that straw.'

'That's that, then. No funny disguises.' Lexi sighed before adding, 'There are other ways, though. We could get the commander to give us another undercover person to be our eyes and ears.'

'It's not the same as having our own eyes and ears. And we'd have to tell him or her what's going on. Bang goes keeping the case quiet. What else have you got?'

'You mentioned surveillance equipment in the car. It's an option,' Lexi said, looking around to make sure none of the other customers were close enough to hear her. 'I could rig the place with hidden cameras and microphones. Almost as good as our own eyes and ears. I could use a bit of help from Terabyte and I definitely need to slip into the community centre before the meeting. Right after this if you want.'

'That's more like it. Better than me in a comedy wig, glasses and moustache.'

'It would have been great to see you … '

'No, it wouldn't.'

Lexi laughed. 'I'll contact Terabyte. That community centre will be like a theatre stage tonight. But none of the actors will know it.'

SCENE 27

Thursday 17th April, Evening

In Shepford Crime Central, Terabyte's long hair flopped forward as he stared down at the controller. Pushing his hair over his shoulders and then his glasses further up his nose, he fine-tuned the receivers. 'Yes,' he announced. 'All microphones and cameras working perfectly. All you need is some people. You'll see everything, hear everything. In fact,' he said, 'you might hear too much. We might have to disentangle the chat if a few conversations go on at the same time. I've got some software that'll do that.'

'Thanks, Terabyte,' said Lexi.

Looking up at the large split-screen of the empty room, Troy nodded. 'Let's get this party started.'

Unaware that they were being monitored, the first members of Two Races Apart filed into the community room at eight twenty-five. Three women and one man, all over fifty years of age, stopped and removed their coats, slipping them over the backs of the seats. They seemed to be in very good spirits. The bugged space was about the size of a classroom, laid out with a few rows of plastic chairs. Tables and sports equipment were stacked against one wall at the far end.

'The system will automatically freeze-frame mug shots,' Lexi told Troy, 'and try to identify the faces against databases.'

'Good, because I don't know any of them,' said Troy.

But he recognized the next person to arrive. It was Precious Austin. She was talking to another woman, complaining about being hounded by police officers.

'Did you tell them about us?' her companion asked.

'No,' Precious lied.

Someone brought in a large tray of hot drinks. There were more mugs of tea than there were people to drink them. Plainly, they expected more arrivals. A different person carried a second tray with a precisely arranged pattern of brightly coloured and chocolate brown cupcakes.

'Mmm,' Troy muttered to himself.

Some more members strolled in and cheerfully greeted the ones already in the community centre. Small groups formed. Tea was drunk. Cupcakes were enjoyed. The last few members joined the group.

In Crime Central, well away from the supporters of Two Races Apart but seeming very close, Lexi said, 'Fourteen altogether. Mostly old folk. I'm sending a message to the commander. Every time the computer identifies someone, we want round-the-clock surveillance on them. And on anyone they meet.'

'That figures.'

The general chatter slowly subsided, the small groups broke up and each member took a seat. At the front, the woman who'd arrived with Precious Austin gave a short celebratory talk. She spent most of her time relishing the news that the Integrated Games had been called off. The rest of the group clapped and cheered wildly. But no one in the room claimed credit for the cancellation. She finished by saying, 'And that's not all. Someone in power has finally come to their senses. Word is out that there's going to be a crackdown on mixed restaurants. No more eating next to tables with filthy insects. No more eating with the disgusting smell of alcohol. Our ideas – the ideas of Two Races Apart – are gaining ground! Small steps towards a bigger, brighter future. It's now time to ramp up the pressure on segregation in hospitals and schools.' The end of her speech was met by further applause, loud and long.

The members of TRAPT broke up once more into clusters. Each group talked about something different. The recent swing towards separation. The weather. Complaints that outers made more demands on the health service because of the way they reproduced. Why separate hospitals were just common sense. The shameful effect of misbehaving young outers on teenage majors.

'Hear that?' Troy said to Terabyte and Lexi. 'You're corrupting me.'

Troy didn't listen to his colleagues' mocking replies. His attention shifted to one particular conversation. A female voice said, 'I wonder what happened to Gritty. I liked him.'

'I saw him this weekend,' an old man replied. 'I don't think he saw me.'

'Where? What was he doing?'

The answer was masked by loud laughter from a nearby collection of members.

Troy cried, 'We need that! What did he say?'

Head down, Terabyte said, 'I'm on the job.'

'Give it some welly.'

Lexi pointed at the output from one of the spy cameras. 'It was them. That bunch of four on the far right.'

'Yeah. I see.'

'It was the old bloke with the stick speaking. Facial recognition hasn't identified him,' Lexi said.

Once the hubbub had died down a bit and Troy could hear the huddle of four again, the subject had changed. They were bemoaning the performance of the local school. 'Not like it was in the good old days when I was there.'

After another thirty seconds, Terabyte announced, 'I've got it. A clever combination of software enhancement and lip-reading. He said, "Sunday night near Shallow End. He was walking along the road." Then they moved to an equally exciting topic.'

'Actually,' Troy replied, 'that *is* quite exciting.' Straightaway, he contacted Commander Cheryl McVeigh's office. 'Troy Goodhart. I need immediate surveillance. I want someone to follow an old fellah home – from the community centre in Shepford's second quarter – and find out who he is. You can't miss him. He's doddery, with a very old-fashioned grey suit, a duffle coat and a wooden walking stick.'

SCENE 28

It turned out that the elderly member of Two Races Apart was Ralph Hester. As Troy walked up the short path to his front door, he said to Lexi. 'This is good. It'll put more wind in our sails.'

'We'll see.'

When the old man opened the door, Troy asked, 'Mr Hester?'

'Yes?'

'Detectives Troy Goodhart and Lexi Four. Can we come in?'

'What's wrong?'

'You may have witnessed a crime on Sunday

evening. We need to know if you can identify the man concerned.'

'Well, I was going to have a shower and go to bed.'

'We won't take long.'

'All right. But are you sure you're detectives? You're so young.'

Troy guessed that, at Ralph Hester's age, almost everyone looked young. In answer, he lifted up his life-logger.

In the living room, which had a faintly unpleasant smell, Troy held up an image of Dominic Varney and asked, 'Do you recognize him?'

'Um, yes. It's Gritty. Well, it's a man I know as Gritty. I don't suppose it's his real name. Mr Gritty doesn't sound right.' Wobbly on his legs, Ralph looked across at Lexi and said, 'Are you an outer, then?'

'Yes. Does it matter?'

The old man merely grunted.

'Do you know where Gritty was on Sunday evening?' Troy asked.

'What's he done?'

'Maybe nothing. To find out, I need to know where he was on Sunday night.'

'Now you mention it, I saw him at Shallow End.'

'Where exactly?' Troy put a street map on his life-logger and held it out for Ralph.

The old man's legs were shaky and unreliable but his shoulders and arms were well developed and strong. His forefinger pointed to a spot just along from the laboratory buildings. 'There. Yes. That's it.'

'Which way was he going?'

'That way.' His finger moved across the screen toward Shallow End Laboratories.

'And what time was this?'

Ralph scratched his head. 'Did you say your name was Goodhart?'

Troy tried to be patient. 'That's right.'

'I went to school with a girl who married a Goodhart. What was her name? Yvonne. That was it. They had a grandson who … I don't know, but there was some funny business. I can't remember … '

'I'm sorry,' Troy said. 'I don't know anyone called Yvonne.' Eager to get back on track, he said, 'Think back to Sunday. What time did you see Gritty?'

'Dear me. I remember more about eighty years ago – with Yvonne at school – than about a few days ago. I don't know for sure but I think it was between half-past seven and eight.'

'Okay. Thanks. That's useful.'

As soon as they left Ralph Hester's house, Lexi turned to her partner and said, 'Dominic Varney near the labs around eight o'clock on Sunday. That's a howling gale in our sails.'

'Yeah. Let's sleep on it.'

'Sleep? If you don't mind, I'll just think about it. And get a search warrant for his house and hut.' She glanced at Troy's lined face and said, 'What's up?'

'He's a colleague,' Troy muttered with a sad shake of his head. 'A police officer.'

'Someone we should be able to trust?'

'Exactly.'

'Nothing's certain yet. Putting him near the crime scene doesn't make him guilty,' Lexi said.

'No. But it's too close for comfort.'

'There's also the issue of whether Hester's reliable. He admitted he's got a shocking memory.'

Troy said, 'But he didn't hesitate much. He was pretty definite. Ancient but believable.'

Lexi smiled. 'He still wasn't a good advert for old age.'

'If I was unkind, I'd say he was in God's waiting room.'

She laughed. 'At his age, he probably likes to think he's going to walk down a tunnel towards a bright light, throw away his walking stick and enter paradise with all the other majors, feeling like a teenager again.'

'What's an outer got to look forward to? Decay or cremation.' Forgetting for a moment a case that had taken an unwelcome turn, Troy said, 'Imagine you're on a plane and the engines fail. There's nothing but ocean all around and you're plunging towards it. You're pretty much guaranteed to die. What do you think about?'

'I wouldn't have time to think,' Lexi replied. 'I'm the pilot, trying to restart the engines.'

'If you were a passenger.'

Lexi shrugged. 'No bright lights. No paradise. My friends? Solved cases? I don't know. I'd be fed up for sure.'

'I'd be content. Comforted by knowing it's part of God's plan for me.'

'What? Huh! You'd be annoyed, angry, scared … '

'No. He'd be taking me home.'

Lexi shook her head in disbelief. Realizing that she wasn't going to shake her partner's faith or get him to admit regret, she switched back to their investigation. 'In a way, it could happen. For outers anyway. If someone releases the soil sample, we'll all be waiting for the crash.'

Abruptly, Troy stopped walking. 'Good point. Right now, nothing much matters, apart from catching whoever's got that vial.'

Lexi also came to a halt. 'You've got some strange ideas, but you care about outers, don't you?'

'All human beings have got an equal right to life.' Troy broke into a smile and said, 'Let's go and mend those engines.'

SCENE 29

Thursday 17th April, Late night

'Yvonne Goodhart?' Troy's grandmother said. 'I haven't heard that name in a while. She's your great-grandma, honey. My mother-in-law. Or she was. Long since gone. Why?'

About to load the plates into the dish washer, Troy hesitated. 'Um ... No reason. Just that an old man I talked to – Ralph Hester – mentioned her.'

Gran shook her head. 'Can't say the name means anything to me. Small world, though.'

'Yes.' Troy placed the plates in the rack and reached for the mugs.

Gran shot a glance at him. 'Did he mention anything else?'

Troy didn't want to share Mr Hester's comment about Yvonne's grandson – his own father – and some funny business. He couldn't face an awkward conversation about his parents. 'No. Not really.'

'You're looking tired.'

'It's a … tricky case.'

'I can see it's bothering you.'

'I haven't bitten off more than I can chew.'

'I'm sure you haven't, honey.'

Troy smiled lamely. 'We might make a bit of progress in the morning.'

'I'm proud of you, young Detective Goodhart. Your mum and dad would be as well.'

Troy nodded. That night, he thought of his parents instead of going to sleep.

SCENE 30

Friday 18th April, Early morning

The sun had been up for only an hour when Lexi got the call. Crime Central still seemed quiet and dominated by outers. Troy had not yet arrived, so Lexi made for the commander's office on her own.

Cheryl McVeigh had hardly got her coat off before checking her overnight messages and deciding to summon Lexi Iona Four.

As soon as Lexi opened the door, Commander McVeigh waved towards her monitor and asked, 'Do you really want to do this?'

Lexi did not need an explanation. She knew that the police chief was referring to her unusual request for a search warrant. 'Yes,' she answered. 'We have good reason … '

'Are you sure you want it known around here that you're targeting a fellow officer?'

'Have you seen the evidence against him?'

'Don't get me wrong. I applaud you for sticking to your principles of going wherever your enquiries take you – especially on this case – but you're asking for trouble when it comes so close to home. You can lose someone's trust in a single moment, but it takes years to get it back.'

Lexi nodded. 'I still want to search Dominic Varney's place.'

'Okay. I'll give you a warrant. Tread carefully, Lexi Four.'

SCENE 31

Panting heavily, Dominic Varney got back to his house just as Troy and Lexi arrived. He was wearing shorts, T-shirt and running shoes. 'Fifteen kilometres,' he said between breaths. He looked at his watch. 'Not bad.' He was almost steaming in the cold morning air.

'We've got a bit of a problem,' Troy told him.

'Have you? What sort of problem?' he gasped.

'A witness who puts you very close to our crime scene – Shallow End Laboratories – at a significant time. Sunday at eight.'

The undercover officer hesitated. He didn't attempt to deny the claim.

'Which means,' Lexi said, 'we've got a search warrant.'

'I know.'

'You know?'

'Word travels fast in the police community. Look, man,' he said. 'I can see how you'd jump to the wrong conclusion about me. I can see it from your point of view. So, I'll talk to you. You've forced me into it. But, if you want it straight, you'll have to agree to ditch the life-loggers – or any other recording devices.'

Intrigued, Lexi and Troy glanced at each other before Troy replied, 'Okay. You've got our attention.'

'I need half an hour for a shower and a quick change.'

'If you can see it from our point of view,' Troy said, 'you'll know we can't leave you for half an hour. That's easily enough time for you to go to your shed or wherever and break open a poison that'll kill Lexi first and then every other outer.'

Dominic sighed. 'What happened to trust among detectives? All right. Come in. Leave all your fancy electronic gadgets inside, let me change – with you watching, if you insist – and we'll go somewhere we can have a private chat. Cloverleaf Park.'

'You're expecting us to postpone the search as well?'

'It's a waste of your time anyway,' Dominic replied. 'Another thing. Just to make sure, I'm bringing a jammer. It'll block all electrical signals. In case of hidden bugs.'

Troy said, 'Sounds like you don't trust us, either.'

'Too right, man.'

While Dominic changed, Lexi took a look at his hut. She didn't have time for a proper search but she saw no evidence of a chemistry laboratory. Most of the space was occupied by garden equipment. In one corner, though, there was a computer and some hi-tech electronic kit. It seemed out of place, but not suspicious.

The park wasn't busy. A woman was jogging around the perimeter and a young man was walking two spaniels. No one took any notice of the three police officers who stopped near the clump of bushes in the middle of the city oasis.

Dominic put down his bag – about the size of a briefcase – and fiddled around inside it. He turned on an electronic jammer. Satisfied, he stood upright and faced the other two detectives. 'If anyone's trying to use a phone or play music within fifty metres, they're out of luck till we're finished.'

'I'm wondering what makes you go to such extremes,' said Troy.

'On Sunday night, I did go past Shallow End Laboratories.'

'You went past?'

'Yes. Not *in*. I went straight past. What's along the road from the laboratories?'

Troy shrugged. 'Quite a few things. Including Shepford Crime Central.'

'Hole in one.' Dominic hesitated and then explained, 'I needed to put a bug and camera where no bug and camera should ever have to be.'

'What?'

'In Shepford Crime Central.'

Troy couldn't resist repeating Dominic's own words. 'Whatever happened to trust among detectives?'

Dominic put up his hands as if surrendering. 'You've got me there. But there's a reason. In Kindale Prison, I was given certain information about Cheryl McVeigh. It's probably – hopefully – just mischief-making, but it was a serious allegation. I felt duty-bound to check it out.'

'So, that's where you were on Sunday night? Bugging the commander's office?'

'That's the real reason I knew about the search warrant.'

'That's not exactly watertight. How are you going to make us believe you?'

'I could tell you the prisoner's name and you could go to Kindale and ask him. Or … ' Looking into Lexi's face, he said, 'You can lose someone's trust in a single moment, but it takes years to get it back.'

Puzzled, Troy gazed at his partner.

Lexi nodded. 'That's word-for-word what Commander McVeigh said to me this morning.'

'Okay. You've wired her office. You've convinced us,' Troy said to Dominic. 'And you wanted this chat off the record in case we're wired as well and the commander's listening in.'

'You have to admit my job's on the line here.'

'But we could just go and tell her. She'd have her office swept and they'll soon find the bugs. So, you'd better tell us what you heard about her. You're going to have to persuade us not to spill the beans.'

'There's a prisoner doing time for fraud. And that's it. He claims he paid Cheryl McVeigh a lot of the proceeds not to investigate a more serious charge of aggravated assault. A bagful of cash got handed over, he says. "You can pay her to bury a case," he told me. "And I'm not the only one." It's possible because she's the commander. She decides what's a priority and what's not. She's the one who chooses where to put person-power.'

For a moment, Troy looked wretched. 'And you want to listen to how she reaches her decisions.'

Interrupting, Lexi added, 'Using the gear in your hut?'

Dominic nodded. 'It's crunch time. There's a case coming up. I know the bad guy. One of his cronies will visit her this afternoon – with plenty of hints about the advantages of downgrading the investigation. I want proof of what's said. I can't rely on either of them to tell the truth after the event. If she opts for the cash incentive, the money will be marked … '

'And, hey presto, you nick the boss for bribery and perverting the course of justice,' said Lexi.

'I hope it's a false alarm. I hope it's just someone with a grudge against her, trying to get her into trouble. But, to find out, I need you two to keep out of it. Let things run their natural course.'

Troy looked at Lexi and asked, 'What do you think?'

'I think it's nothing to do with us. We've got enough to worry about without getting distracted by something else.' She paused and then quoted Troy, 'Nothing matters much, apart from catching the person with the vial.'

Troy nodded slowly, thoughtfully. To Dominic, he said, 'I guess this conversation never took place. But … '

'What?'

'Did you see anyone outside the labs at Shallow End when you went past? Anything suspicious?'

Dominic drew a deep breath. 'I don't think so. There were a few cars, moving and parked. I wasn't the only one on foot, either. A woman maybe and a man with a walking stick. I didn't see either of them from the front and it was pretty dark. Anyway, I wasn't paying attention. I was thinking ahead.'

'Would you recognize the woman if I showed you a photo?'

Dominic laughed. 'No chance. I didn't see her face.'

'Was she tall? Short? What was she wearing?'

'You're desperate for evidence, aren't you? There was nothing unusual about her. Otherwise, I'd remember. She wasn't enormously tall, incredibly short or anything. She was near the main gates, I think.' He shrugged. 'That's your lot, man.'

Once they'd retrieved their life-loggers from Dominic's house, Troy said to his partner, 'The spotlight's shifted, but he's not completely in the clear, you know. His version still isn't watertight. Even if he went to Crime Central on Sunday, it doesn't mean he didn't drop in at the labs first. Unlikely, but not impossible.'

'I know. So, what's your gut telling you?'

'I don't get the impression he's been radicalized against outers. And if he isn't, what's his motive?' Troy shrugged and then smiled. 'We've got evidence against him, but the pole we're trying to climb is too greasy. It doesn't want to be climbed.'

SCENE 32

Troy and Lexi sifted through the information on the TRAPT supporters who had been identified by computer. Apart from Precious Austin, they did not know any of them, but now they were all being monitored furtively 24 hours a day. The woman who had given the talk on Thursday night – the leader of Two Races Apart perhaps – was a major called Oriana Skillicorn. She was a decorator and interior designer and she did not have a criminal record. She also had nothing to do with science, biohazards and Shallow End Laboratories.

In Precious Austin's familiar living room, Troy

held out a head-and-shoulders photograph of Oriana Skillicorn and asked, 'Do you know this woman?'

Precious crinkled her face as if concentrating. 'I don't think so. No.'

'That's weird,' Troy replied, 'because you were seen with her last night.'

'Let me have another look.' Pretending to reconsider the mug shot, Precious said, 'Ah. Yes. Sorry. It's Oriana. I didn't recognize her at first.'

Trying not to become tetchy straightaway, Troy said with a smirk, 'Yes. I understand. It's been hours since you last saw her.'

'No,' Precious replied. 'It's just that … Anyway, it's Oriana Skillicorn.'

'Another member of Two Races Apart?'

'Yes, I believe so.'

'I tried to get to your meeting last night,' Troy said, 'but I couldn't make it. Was it a good one?'

Wary, Precious answered, 'It was okay. Nothing special.'

Troy sprung a surprise. 'We want to look around your house.'

'Why?'

'To see what's in it. It's not a search. Nothing formal. Just a quick peek inside each room. And Lexi would like to see all your blouses.'

'What for?'

'To check out the cuffs. You know. The ones held together by buttons.'

Precious grimaced. 'I don't like them. They make the end of the sleeves too much of a feature. I don't have a single top with a cuff.'

'So, you don't mind us taking a look around?'

'Can I refuse?'

'Yes. You're within your rights to give us the impression that you've got something to hide.'

Precious snorted. 'I can't really, then.'

'Thanks,' Troy said. 'We won't take long.'

It seemed to be true that Precious Austin did not have any tops with cuffs on the sleeves. 'Unless,' Lexi pointed out, 'she realized what she'd done and destroyed the evidence. Or maybe it's in the laundry.'

The house had a simple layout. Troy and Lexi checked every room for signs of a laboratory. They found none until they reached the extension built out from the kitchen. It was one large whitewashed and windowless room that housed all of her honey-making apparatus. There were shelves with bottles and jars, some empty and some full of amber fluid. Two wooden boxes containing unused empty frames were pushed against one wall. There was a large stainless steel extractor and two filtration units with steel meshes. On the floor were stacks of spotless plastic pots. Perhaps it was too early in the season for production to be in full swing. On another shelf, there were latex gloves, overalls, aprons, hair-nets, a camera and coiled tubing. The ceiling had a generous array of LED lamps.

In a way, the room was a laboratory, but no vial of poison was on view. Only a thorough search would reveal whether the space put aside for processing honey was doubling up as a place to manipulate a dangerous biohazard. And that would require a warrant.

SCENE 33

Troy looked at Lexi's monitor and said, 'It's like a spider's web.'

'Eh? That'd be one crazy spider.'

Troy was sifting through the digital and telephone reports from the officers who were tailing the members of Two Races Apart, but Lexi had converted the same information into a diagram.

'Look,' she said. 'It's simple. Even you will get this. There's a circle of thirteen dots. Each dot is a TRAPT supporter. I put Oriana Skillicorn at the centre because she seems to be the leader. Each dot is connected to every other because they all got together last night. Every time one of them meets or contacts someone new, I add another dot outside the main circle and draw in a new line between them. It's good because if they all start contacting the same person, you see it straightaway. Lots of lines start converging on one dot. Or,' Lexi said with a smile, 'as you'd put it, the spider starts a new web. It's a nice visual way of seeing if there's a key player.'

'Okay. It beats going through updates on fourteen different people, looking for common factors. I'll give you that.'

Some TRAPT supporters – like Ralph Hester and Precious Austin – had stayed at home since the meeting and had hardly gained any extra strands. Others – like Oriana Skillicorn – had gone to a workplace and come into contact with so many people that it was impractical or impossible to show their entire networks.

'It's the methodical way of doing things. Over here,' Lexi said, pointing to the left of her screen, 'are four more dots. They're our other suspects. Saul Tingle, Fern Mountstephen, Eric Kiss and Dominic Varney. If any of them get in touch with one of the TRAPT brigade, it'd make a very significant and noticeable line.'

'The spider would go off at a tangent.'

'We'll see.'

They both groaned as a new message arrived. They were both required in the commander's office without delay.

Before they left, Lexi asked another officer to monitor the surveillance team's reports and to update the on-screen graphic.

Lexi and Troy found themselves standing in front of Cheryl McVeigh's deputy. He looked up at them and said, 'In case you're wondering, I've been appointed Temporary Commander.'

'What happened to Commander McVeigh?' Lexi asked.

'There'll be an enquiry and an announcement in due course, I dare say,' her replacement told them. 'But she resigned unexpectedly this afternoon – with immediate effect.'

Troy nodded. It was not difficult to guess. Dominic Varney had been right – and he'd exposed her corruption. Rather than resisting, trying to squirm her way out of the mess, Cheryl McVeigh had stepped down at once.

'Now, as to more important things … I'm overseeing your case personally,' the new commander said. 'I'm reassessing the situation. First, as I understand it, you haven't carried out a thorough search of Dominic Varney's address. Why not?'

The two detectives glanced at each other and came to the same unspoken conclusion. They decided not to reveal what they knew about Dominic Varney's part in the previous commander's downfall.

'I ... er ... thought about what Commander McVeigh said about trust in each other,' Lexi answered, 'and changed my mind. We talked to him instead. But we can go back if we need to. The warrant's still valid.'

'That could be seen as the actions of a young and indecisive team.' The commander gazed at Lexi and then shifted his eyes towards Troy. 'Why haven't you arrested Precious Austin? She seems to have guilt tattooed across her forehead.'

Troy coughed. 'Just because she's low-hanging fruit doesn't make her the bad apple.'

The new commander gazed at him with open disdain. 'What?'

'She's too high profile. Going out vandalising property is not the way our guy would operate. He might be dancing to her tune – or Oriana Skillicorn's tune – but I'm sure he'll be keeping a low profile.'

The commander stared again at Lexi. 'You're a bit

more experienced, Lexi Four. Have you told your partner it's about evidence?'

'I don't need to. He knows that. But I trust his instinct as well.'

'Ah. Troy Goodhart's famous perceptiveness.' He smiled unkindly and then added, 'I can't agree with Commander McVeigh's – *ex*-Commander McVeigh's – approach to this investigation. I am going to put it in the hands of an experienced officer. You two will continue under his or her instructions, as part of a new team. It may take me until morning to speak to and organize the best people. Until then, continue. Dismissed.'

Walking along the corridor towards their room in the forensic department of Shepford Crime Central, Lexi muttered, 'That's that, then.'

'I'm not entirely surprised,' Troy said. 'Maybe I was more surprised when Cheryl McVeigh let us keep such a scary case. We are … quite new to this game.'

'Huh. What's an older guy going to do that we haven't?'

Feeling glum, Troy shrugged.

'Arrest Precious Austin,' Lexi suggested.

'Sounds like it, but … '

'I know. Commanders like arrests. Makes them think they're getting somewhere.'

Troy smiled sadly. 'I think Precious Austin's best left alone – with someone tailing her to see what she does. That's much more likely to get results than locking her up in an interview room.'

In less than a minute, Troy was proved right. As soon as they entered their room, their eyes went to the monitor. In their absence, Lexi's helper had drawn in new lines on the matrix. Two of them veered to the left and met on one particular dot, one particular suspect from Shallow End Laboratories, proving a connection between three people. Precious Austin and Oriana Skillicorn had both met with the same suspect. The two lines were attached to Fern Mountstephen's dot, as if trying to drag her into the complex web.

'That's not all.' Examining her life-logger, Lexi said, 'We've got the bad guy's next message.'

3RD demand.
Different bodies **NEED** *different*
MEDICINE. Do *away* **with** *mixed*
HOSPITALS.

'Hospitals,' Troy murmured. Then he nodded and

said to himself, 'Definitely dancing to someone else's tune.'

SCENE 34

Friday 18th April, Night

'But she's hardly been on the radar,' Lexi said, on the way to intercept Fern Mountstephen, one of the technicians from Shallow End Laboratories. 'She's got a cast-iron alibi. She was at a gym on Sunday evening.'

'Yeah,' Troy agreed. Then he added, 'I'm thinking that through.'

'She was a Friend to the Integrated Games.'

'I'm going to ask her about that.'

Lexi sighed and changed tack. 'It's a bit of a coincidence that Oriana Skillicorn talked about targeting hospitals at the meeting last night and today ... '

'Exactly. The third demand to segregate hospitals. But it doesn't make her our murderer for certain. For one thing, she's not enough of a scientist. But someone else might be doing her bidding. Someone who heard her TRAPT talk or someone she's met since. Somebody who knows enough science.'

'Like Fern Mountstephen?'

'Maybe.'

'Or it really could be a coincidence.'

Troy smiled. 'You don't believe that.'

'No.'

Troy and Lexi heard the loud snarls and growls from the stadium even before they entered. 'You wouldn't want to live near it, would you?' said Troy, almost shouting above the racket.

'I wouldn't mind,' Lexi yelled back. 'It gets the adrenalin going.'

They had been informed by the surveillance team that both Precious Austin and Fern Mountstephen were at Shepford Speedway. As they went in, the revving of motorcycles became deafening. The tapes went up and four bikes hurtled down the oval track. Under floodlights, the riders slid round the first corner almost sideways, tyres kicking up clouds of orangey-brown dirt.

'Let's walk round till we see her,' Troy yelled at his partner.

Lexi did not shift her eyes from the race. She merely nodded.

Troy imagined he'd have to hold Lexi back from grabbing a bike and having a go.

The speedway riders went anti-clockwise four times around the sand-coloured track. The race was all over in just over one minute and, for a while, the noise level eased. But the next four riders were already appearing from the tunnel. Engines soon began to snarl again. As Troy and Lexi moved through the crowd, another contest began and one of the motorcycles threw up particularly dense clouds of dirt over the spectators at both ends of the stadium as it broadsided into the bends.

Lexi looked down and noticed that orange specks had settled on the sleeve of her coat. She nudged her partner and pointed out the stain.

Troy nodded. There was a lull in the proceedings and he took advantage of the quiet to speak without shouting. 'Same colour as the marks on that piece of cardboard.'

'Like grains of sand,' Lexi said. 'Whoever arranged the second demand might have taken the dirt home from here.'

There seemed to be an interval in the tournament. The two detectives weaved through the spectators more quickly. Without the distraction of the speedway heats, Lexi paid more attention to faces in the crowd.

They spotted Fern Mountstephen in the east stand with a group of friends, all sipping hot drinks from plastic cups. Judging by the smell, some contained alcohol. Precious Austin was not among them. When Fern noticed the detectives, her expression changed rapidly from merriment to displeasure.

'Sorry to interrupt,' Troy said, 'but we need a chat. It'd be better to go somewhere … quieter. More private.'

Fern groaned but agreed. Coat spattered with grime from the track, she led them to the stadium café which was almost deserted. Clearly, spectators had made their way back to trackside in anticipation of the next round of races.

They sat down at a table and Troy began. 'How did you get on with Precious Austin when she was still working at the labs?'

Fern shrugged. 'Okay, I guess.'

'Have you seen her since?'

'Now and again, yes.'

'Here tonight?'

She hesitated for an instant. 'No.'

'When was the last time?' Troy asked.

'Earlier this evening, as it happens.'

Outside, engines began to rev up once more.

'What about Oriana Skillicorn?'

'She was with Precious. In the restaurant down the road.'

'I'm guessing it was a major-only one?'

'As it turns out, yes.'

'Did you eat with them?'

'No. I was just there. We didn't arrange to meet. I sat with them for a few minutes – just to be social, you know. They're a bit … '

'What?'

'Prejudiced. Against outers.'

'And you're not?' said Troy.

'Didn't you see my friends?' She nodded towards the east stand. 'Two majors and five outers.'

'You're quick to tell me that. Why do you think I'd be interested?'

'Because you're investigating a major versus outer thing. It's got nothing to do with me because I like outers. Obviously.'

Troy pretended to be puzzled. 'Hang on. You think you're a suspect. Why?'

'Because, as it happens, you're questioning me.'

Troy smiled. 'We don't confine ourselves to suspects. Most of the time, we talk to people with useful information.'

Fern looked doubtful. 'What do you want to know?'

'You were a Friend to the Integrated Games. What was that all about?'

'I thought it would be a good thing to support. I don't know what I was going to be asked to do. It would've been some sort of stewarding job.'

To Troy, it seemed like an easy way to deflect suspicion by appearing to approve of the mixing of majors and outers.

Four noisy engines revved simultaneously as the next heat got underway.

Troy asked, 'Do you come here a lot?'

'Quite a lot. It's really exciting. When you're allowed to watch.'

'Can Lexi see the sleeve of your blouse – or whatever? Just pull the coat up a bit.'

Fern did as he asked and Lexi took a photograph of the buttoned cuff.

'What's this about?'

Lexi said, 'I'm going to need to see all your tops.'

'As it turns out, I didn't bring them all with me,' Fern replied with venom.

Lexi ignored the sarcasm. 'No problem. We can go back to your place.'

'But … ' Disappointed, she glanced in the direction of the track.

'We're investigating three murders,' Troy said. 'I think that trumps a night out with mates at speedway.'

Fern sighed. 'I suppose so.'

SCENE 35

'Well?' Troy whispered impatiently in Fern Mountstephen's bedroom.

'There's one here,' Lexi told him quietly as she completed the recognition analysis on her life-logger. 'It's a buttoned cuff from one of her blouses and it's as good a match as Dominic Varney's. Both fall within error limits.'

'And she could easily have dropped a couple of specks from the speedway track onto the card. She said she goes a lot.'

'It's brick granules, apparently,' Lexi told him. 'That means clay to me. But ... '

'What?'

Unsure how much Fern would be able to hear from downstairs, Lexi kept her voice quiet. 'She's got all these outer friends.'

'She comes across as friendly but, behind that, there's something severe about her. Are they really friends or is she acting – like Dominic Varney?'

'You're not convincing me.'

'I reckon our guy keeps a low profile. She fits. She doesn't go to TRAPT meetings, doesn't spray graffiti on walls, and she stays close to outers. That could all be wool she's pulling over our eyes, so she looks way south of guilty.'

'Huh. Having a good alibi for Sunday night keeps her profile very low.'

Troy nodded. 'I've asked Terabyte to go through every bit of the Shallow End computer. All night, if he needs it. I want him to find out exactly what happened last Sunday at about eight o'clock.'

'What's on your mind?'

'Probably nothing. I just think we could use some Terabyte magic. For now,' he said, 'we need to know if she's got a secret lab in here somewhere. With a vial, sticky tape that oozes acid, and bits of card with messages spelled out on them.'

'I'll send an emergency request for a search

warrant to our lovely new commander. Maybe it'll get him out of bed.' She smiled and added, 'I hope so.'

'Our reason's flimsy, but the stakes are so high he's got to give us permission. Hasn't he?'

Lexi shrugged. 'We'll see.'

The temporary commander disagreed. His message was plain. *There's far greater reason to issue a search warrant for Precious Austin's house than Fern Mountstephen's.*

While Troy talked to Fern, the best that Lexi could do was to download the plan for the original building. And the first thing to catch her eye was that the main schematic showed a cellar.

Fern was complaining, 'You've just invaded my wardrobe … '

'With your permission,' Troy stressed.

'Now you want to poke around everywhere else! Don't you need some sort of warrant … ?'

'That's if we wanted to be thorough and, if necessary, break things open. We just want to take a quick look. You can give us permission to do that. You can escort us, if you want. I don't know why you'd refuse, unless you've got something to hide.'

'It's getting late.'

Troy smiled. 'I bet you'd still be at the speedway if it wasn't for us.'

Fern sighed wearily and then said, 'All right. Come on. I'll take you upstairs again and work our way down.'

'Thanks. It's good of you,' Troy replied, following her.

Ten minutes later, having peered into every room and explored her garden shed by torchlight, they were no wiser.

Lexi said, 'There's one place you haven't shown us.'

'Oh?' Fern seemed surprised.

'This house has a basement.'

'Does it? Well, I've lived here for four years as it happens and I haven't seen one.' She spread her arms. 'I mean, where is it?'

The plan of the building didn't help. The place where there was supposed to be access to the cellar had long since been bricked up and become part of a cloakroom.

'I think we've come to a dead end,' Troy admitted. 'Nothing else we can do unless we get a search warrant.'

Looking relieved, Fern showed the detectives to the door.

Walking away, Troy said, 'We'll put her under the closest possible surveillance overnight. I don't want her to go to the toilet without us knowing.'

Lexi screwed up her nose. 'Not a pleasant image.' Then she added, 'I'm going to analyse that third demand.'

Troy nodded. 'Good. I'm going to have a think and, if I can, catch a nowhere-near-enough amount of sleep. Then … who knows?'

Lexi glanced at him. 'You want this sorted out first thing in the morning.'

'Don't you?'

'Sure,' Lexi replied. 'It'd be good to wrap this bit up neatly for the new investigator.'

Troy's smile was grim. 'I'd rather hand over a solved case with nothing to do but charge the bad guy.'

Lexi shook her head. 'I'm not sure we're even close.'

SCENE 36

Saturday 19th April, Early hours

Saul Tingle had not left Shallow End Laboratories. He sat with Julia Neve Nineteen in the computer room and watched the scruffy young man from Shepford Crime Central as his fingers flew across a keypad, delving deeper and deeper into the programming.

Neither of them knew enough about computers to figure out what he was doing. They had to trust him. But both of them were anxious. This man – almost a boy – could cripple the workings of the laboratories if he deleted or altered one line of the intricate operating system.

Terabyte turned round, pushed his hair behind his

ears and said, 'Any chance of a beer to keep me going? This is thirsty work.'

Julia nodded. 'I'll take care of it.' She left the room.

'You don't have to watch me, you know,' Terabyte said. 'I'd probably finish quicker if I didn't have spectators.'

'Nervous spectators,' Saul replied. 'I'm here because I need to see that the system's okay for next week. It's vital to our safety and our entire business.'

'I know,' Terabyte replied as he got back to work. 'You've made that point three times already. I'm treating it with respect. It's a bit flabby, though.'

'Flabby?'

'Yeah. There's the original set of instructions and hundreds of additions. Patches on patches. Really, you want to scrap the lot and start again from scratch. Keep it tight and neat. It'll be faster and more reliable that way.'

'I think we won't touch it just yet,' Saul replied. 'Not while we've got … other things on our minds.' He thought he heard a noise and he glanced at the door.

'It self-checks,' Terabyte told him. 'When I'm finished, I'll run a system-wide scan to make sure it's as good as it can be.'

'Good.' But Saul still looked tense.

When Julia came back in with a large glass of dark ale for Terabyte, the unit director nearly jumped out of his chair.

'Only me,' she said.

Saul wiped some sweat from his brow. 'I'm not used to working through the night. It's quiet. Creepy.'

Terabyte downed half the beer in a single swig and then continued to delve into the complex codes.

It was an hour and a half later – just after he'd finished his third beer – when he sat back and said, 'That's it! I need to talk to Lexi and Troy.'

Saul jolted upright. 'What about? What have you found?'

'First,' Terabyte replied, 'I need to talk to them in private.' He got up and left the computer room to find a place where he could call his colleagues in confidence.

Still drowsy, Troy sat on the edge of his bed and listened carefully. In Crime Central, Lexi was much more alert as she took part in the three-cornered conversation.

'Right. I don't know if this is what you'd got in mind, Troy, but there's a difference in the way the lab's computer recorded Sunday night's raid into the high-security lab. Normally, when someone goes through all those decontamination chambers, the software enters the time and date automatically in one type of format. I've gone back over weeks of data and it's always the same. When the first door opens, the time gets recorded to the nearest tenth of a second. I don't know why – it's not necessary – but that's what the system does. You get an entry like 09:55:17.2. Last Sunday, the door opened at 19:58:00.0 and, on the way out, it was 20:32:00.0. Now, what are the chances that someone went in and came out exactly on the nearest minute? Not even missing it by a tenth of a second.'

Troy shivered. He had begun to suspect trickery and Terabyte's discovery made him wish he'd checked before.

Lexi said, 'You're suggesting someone entered the time and date manually – to the nearest minute – and the computer filled in the missing figures with zeroes.'

'I can't think of any other explanation,' Terabyte replied.

'So the doors didn't open at all. Someone just made it look like they did.'

'Good work,' said Troy. 'Exactly what you'd expect if someone wanted to provide themselves with a perfect alibi for Sunday night.'

Terabyte laughed. 'That's what's let them down. The times are too perfect.'

Without wasting another moment, Troy said, 'Let's find out where Blaine Twenty-Two is, Lexi. I'll meet you there.'

SCENE 37

Saturday 19th April, Pre-dawn

Outside one of Shepford's schools, Troy looked at his approaching partner and, puzzled, said, 'School? At three in the morning?'

Lexi nodded. 'I'm guessing it's a Blossoming.'

'I've heard of that.'

'Bringing up an outer baby is a job for a nanny. Seeing them to adulthood – at the age of fourteen for us – is a job for the community. When they reach it, the community celebrates with a Blossoming.'

'But at three in the morning?'

'Apart from a few fifteen-minute pauses, we're twenty-four hours a day people, remember. And we prefer to do it when most majors aren't around. In fact,' she said, 'it's probably best for you to wait here and I'll go in and get Blaine.'

'Majors not welcome, eh?'

'You'd be ... a distraction.' Lexi smiled and went towards the entrance on her own.

When she brought out the technician from Shallow End Laboratories, Troy was in a hurry. Standing in the light of the school's reception, he said, 'Think back to last Friday. Your end-of-the-week maintenance visit to BSL4 with Fern Mountstephen. Who left the lab first? Who was first into decontamination?'

'Er ... me.'

'So, Fern was behind you. For a while, you couldn't see what she was doing.'

'No. But it wasn't long. Well, longer than normal now I think about it, but not a huge wait.'

'Did you take anything in with you?'

'A specially designed bag for new equipment needed in the lab,' said Blaine.

'Both of you had one?'

'Yes. Why?'

Troy ignored the question. He nodded knowingly. At last, he had a mental picture of what had happened. 'Thanks,' he said. But before leaving, he asked one more question. 'By the way, is Fern hot with computers?'

'Better than me – and probably better than most majors,' Blaine answered.

As they raced back to Fern Mountstephen's house, Lexi said to her partner, 'I haven't got much on that third demand. No more impressions, but there was something that could've been a particle of clay.' She paused and then turned to make eye contact with him. 'I was worried that you'd hold me back – like a lot of majors, but … '

'Yes?'

'Looks like you've called another one right.'

'Maybe. Fern was the last person out of the lab on Friday. When Blaine turned his back to leave, she released some SUMP and put the vial in her bag. If she contaminated them both in the process, the poison was destroyed as they came through the cleaning stages. Then she tinkered with the computer, making it look like a Sunday sabotage while she was at the gym.'

'Hey presto. A clever alibi.'

'Not quite clever enough.'

'You know,' Lexi said, 'there's a chance we might just sort this out before sun's up and we get relegated.'

'It's our bike,' Troy replied. 'We don't want anyone else pedalling it. But what I really want is someone in a cell and that vial of SUMP back in BSL4.'

In their final few minutes before confronting Fern Mountstephen, they consulted the surveillance team. Apparently, she was upstairs in her bedroom with the light out, almost certainly asleep. They also studied the plans of her house on Lexi's life-logger.

Frustrated, Troy shook his head. 'There must be a way into her basement.'

Lexi nodded, thinking about the layout. Her forefinger followed the lines and angles, and came to a stop at the place that was now a cloakroom. 'It's still got to be here somewhere. It can't be anywhere else.'

'It fits. But … ' He shrugged.

'A false floor,' Lexi said. 'We're looking for a trapdoor.'

Outside Fern's home, Lexi whispered, 'Everything's changed. Now the evidence has built up, we can break in if we're sure someone's in danger or if we can prevent a serious crime.'

Troy nodded. 'Every outer's in danger and killing them all's a pretty serious crime.'

'Agreed,' Lexi said. 'I don't think we need an

invitation or a warrant. We're going in.' Her right foot crashed into the door.

With a ring of surveillance officers outside to make sure the suspect could not escape, Troy and Lexi went in search of conclusive proof. They made straight for the cloakroom. Lexi dropped to her knees and rummaged near the carpet. It wasn't properly fixed to the floorboards. Rolling it back, she revealed a concealed hatch. 'Hey presto,' she whispered. 'No dust. Not musty. This is used a lot.' She levered up the trapdoor with her fingernails and revealed steps descending into a black hole. She didn't wait. She put her left foot on the first step and at once lights came on to guide her. 'Controlled by a motion detector,' she said.

She led the way down into a makeshift laboratory with a smooth concrete floor.

Careful not to touch or disturb anything, the two detectives recorded it all on their life-loggers. To the right was a fume cupboard. On the left, there was a long bench with various flasks, tubes, beakers, syringes and other chemical equipment. Further along was a digital camera capable of recording video. There was also a small roll of sticky tape.

'I'll have to analyse it,' Lexi said quietly, 'but it looks familiar.'

'Looks like a trump card to me.'

In the far corner, there was a cubicle that looked like a shower unit. But it was more sophisticated. It was, perhaps, Fern's amateurish version of a high-security lab.

Troy pointed to a piece of cardboard on a shelf next to the chamber. It was another threat.

4th demand.
Major *schools* and separate *OUTER* schools. *Do* **AWAY** *with* **MIXED** schools.

'Not the final piece of the jigsaw,' Troy said, 'but enough to convict.'

Lexi nodded, still anxious. 'But where's the final piece?'

'Looking for this?'

They both spun round to see Fern Mountstephen standing on the stairs, holding up a glass vial.

'I took the precaution of scoring the glass,' she told them. 'It's weakened. Just a tap and it'll break.'

Troy stepped forward. What he did next and what he said next would decide the fate of every outer. Trying to control his emotions, he said, 'I don't think you want this on your conscience, Fern. Someone would have to invent a new term for what you're thinking of doing. It's north of ethnic cleansing, worse than genocide.'

'There's already a word for it. Extinction.'

'Is that what you want to be remembered for?'

'I dare say you've got the place surrounded. Let me go, clear me a way through and no one'll die. Get me a cab and I'll leave this,' she said, nodding at the vial, 'by the side of the road.'

At once, Troy shook his head. 'I can't do that. For lots of reasons. For one thing, I can't trust you to leave it. You could get in the car and throw it from the window.'

'You have to trust me.'

'Why would I do that?'

'Because I have to trust you not to rig the cab to take me straight to Crime Central.'

'No.'

She gripped the vial in both hands, ready to snap it into two pieces.

'No!' he shouted.

'A cab, then,' Fern said.

Troy took a step towards her and then hesitated. 'Let me check something on my life-logger.'

Immediately suspicious, Fern said, 'What are you doing?'

'It's a big call for me and Lexi. I'm asking our commander if he'll offer you a deal.'

'Under these circumstances, what choice has he got?'

'It'll take a few minutes.' Troy looked up at her and said, 'Think of your friends. Outer friends.'

Fern screwed up her face. 'They weren't friends. They were insurance, so I didn't look like a separatist. Sick of the sight of them all.'

Playing for time, Troy said, 'What's the problem with outers, Fern?'

'Don't you know what it's like to work with them, live alongside them, go to school with them? Always claiming to be superior to you.'

'They're better than me at some things, not as good at others. That's okay.'

'At school, I had a friend – a *real* friend. A major. They – outers – made fun of her all the time. It was relentless. Until she snapped.'

Troy allowed her a moment of silence.

'I was the one who found her hanging from her bedroom door.'

'I'm sorry,' Troy said softly. 'That's awful. It must have been a terrible shock. But you can't blame every outer for a few rogue bullies. You can't condemn them all. Lexi wouldn't have done anything like that to your friend.'

'I would have tried my best to stop it,' said Lexi.

Troy took another two steps towards the technician. 'You can't take it out on Lexi and all the others who'd be horrified by what happened. That's not fair.'

'But they just keep digging away. "We're cleverer than you." Well, they've dug enough to make themselves a great big grave.'

'What was your friend's name?'

'Celine.'

'Is that what Celine would have wanted? The extinction of outers.'

'After what she went through, yes.' Fern looked down at him and hissed, 'Don't come any closer. What has your boss said?'

'Nothing yet,' Troy replied. 'He's a major. Probably asleep. Someone will get him on task as soon as possible.'

'It had better be soon.'

Troy looked again at his life-logger and came to a decision. 'Here's the thing, Fern. I'm not as clever as most outers. I admit it. But I think I know people. I think I know you.'

Her hands tightened on the glass container. Her knuckles were white. 'What are you talking about?'

'I don't think you'll do it, Fern. I don't think you'll

kill every outer. That's why I checked something.' He motioned towards his life-logger.

'You weren't consulting your boss?'

'No. I'm looking at images of glass vials. And I've got a dilemma. That one in your hand isn't the same as the one in the video about the Integrated Games. It's different from the photos in the other two demands. And I don't think it's the same as the ones our drone picked out in BSL4.'

Fern swallowed and said, 'That's because I transferred the SUMP to this one.'

'In here?' Troy looked around at the facilities – far more crude than Shallow End Laboratories. 'I'm a long way south of outers when it comes to science as well, but I think that'd be too risky.' He glanced at Lexi and she nodded her nervous agreement. 'And I don't know why you'd change one sealed bottle for another.' Troy walked forward two more paces until he was at the bottom of the stairs.

'Get back!' she yelled.

Troy mounted the first step. 'It'd be better if you handed it over to me, Fern.'

There was a loathing in Fern's face.

Troy knew her expression wasn't aimed at outers this time. In that instant, she loathed him. Because he'd figured it out. He went up another step.

And that triggered her. She raised the vial over her head and threw it down onto the hard floor where it smashed into three pieces. Something that looked like soil spilled out.

At once, Fern turned and flew back up the stairs.

Troy let her go. The team outside would deal with her. He had more important work.

Lexi came to his side and said, 'I hope you're right, Troy.'

He got down and photographed the main part of the broken container and immediately sent the image to Julia Nineteen. Talking to Lexi while he made the phone call, he said, 'She's an outer. She'll be up.' As soon as the laboratory supervisor answered, Troy said, 'Well? Is that your vial – in pieces?'

There was deathly quiet for five seconds.

Troy was sweating and the silence seemed like a lifetime to Lexi.

Then Julia's voice said, 'No. No, it isn't.'

Troy replied, 'Thanks. That's what I thought as well.' He ended the call and turned to his partner. 'She was bluffing, trying to make her escape. That's all.'

'So, where's the real vial? I can't see it here.'

Troy took a deep breath. 'I don't know, but she met up with Precious Austin and Oriana Skillicorn so I'm guessing … '

Lexi checked her life-logger. 'You might be right,' she said, the dread clear in her tone. 'I'm getting reports that all the tailed TRAPT members are getting up early. Skillicorn's already heading in the direction of the community centre.'

'As if they've got something new and urgent to talk about. Like a way of killing all outers.'

'We can listen. I haven't removed the bugs and cameras yet.'

Troy said, 'We've got to do more than listen.' He made another call. This time, he had to be patient.

While he waited for the ringing to wake Dominic Varney, Lexi whispered, 'They've arrested Fern Mountstephen upstairs.'

Troy nodded. 'We'll charge her on our way out.'

Dominic's voice, barely recognizable with drowsiness, said, 'Yes?'

'Troy Goodhart. I need you right now, Dominic. I'm delegating to you – to Gritty really – the job of saving every outer on the planet.'

SCENE 38

Saturday 19th April, Dawn

Masking the first light of dawn, the black cloud overhead unleashed a torrent of rain on Troy and Lexi as they huddled under some trees outside the entrance to the community centre, watching the events inside on their life-loggers.

Making his way through the downpour, Dominic Varney approached the main door. Troy and Lexi stood up so that he could see that they were already in position. Dominic glanced across at his colleagues and, totally immersed in his role of bigot, he shouted abuse at Lexi before he entered.

Oriana Skillicorn was on her feet, standing in front

of three rows of believers in the ideas of Two Races Apart. When Gritty walked in, dripping water from his raincoat, there was a commotion and a disruption. But he seemed to be welcome.

'I heard you were getting together,' he said in a loud voice. 'Strange time to do it, so I reckoned something big had come up. I didn't want to miss out.'

Oriana waved him towards a seat. 'It doesn't come any bigger.' She clutched a vial and lifted it up. 'A poison that doesn't affect majors. A poison that kills only outers. All outers. It gives us incredible power and incredible responsibility. Right now, we could banish outers to hell forever. We alone could inherit the Earth.'

The reaction from the TRAPT supporters was hard to gauge from outside in a noisy April shower. Troy and Lexi guessed that a majority – including Gritty – were calling for the extermination of outers. A few were shaking their heads. Perhaps they had their quibbles with outers but a terrible, irreversible revenge was simply too much for them to sanction. Some were cheering. Ralph Hester was waving his walking stick in the air.

Precious called out, 'Let's go for it. We – majors – can fill the holes they'd leave behind. All it takes is a bit of learning and a lot of determination.'

Gritty glanced around at them all and then shouted above the mayhem, 'Let's have a vote.'

Troy said to his partner, 'He's making sure we've got pictures – proof – of who's in favour of mass murder and who isn't.'

Rainwater ran down their faces and necks and seeped into their clothes but neither Troy nor Lexi noticed the discomfort. Hearts pounding, they were focused entirely on the meeting. They were focused on the future of outers. They had also steeled themselves in case there came a moment when they'd have to decide whether to storm the meeting.

Precious got to her feet. 'I agree. It's the only way.'

'All right,' Oriana said. 'Let's do it. First, hands up … '

'It should be a secret ballot,' someone shouted.

Outside, Troy muttered a curse.

'We can't organize that here and now,' Gritty argued. 'It's a waste of time, man.'

There seemed to be general acceptance that a formal vote was going too far.

'Okay. A show of hands. Put your hand up if you want to save outers.' Oriana paused for a second or two and then counted the raised hands. 'Now, hands up for casting them out for all eternity.' Again she counted.

The members of Two Races Apart didn't need to wait for Oriana's announcement. They'd seen the decision of the majority for themselves. Even so, they gazed at her.

'If you include my vote, it's ten in favour of releasing the poison and five against.'

More applause.

'You're all welcome to stay,' she told the meeting, 'but some of you – five – might want to leave now.'

Three got to their feet straightaway. The remaining two were going to stay but, on seeing the others grab their coats, they followed suit.

Lexi and Troy ducked down, making sure they were out of sight when the five objectors traipsed out of the community centre.

'Now,' Oriana said, 'if we're going to go ahead with this, one of us has got to break the vial.'

'She's a coward as well,' Troy muttered. 'She doesn't want to do it herself.'

'We should draw lots,' Ralph suggested.

'It's one possibility,' she replied.

'She won't agree to that,' Lexi said with a sneer. 'She might get the short straw and be forced to do it.'

'It's just like the secret ballot,' Gritty replied. 'Too much trouble. And I don't know about you but I'm completely out of straws.'

'What are you suggesting?' Precious asked.

'A volunteer,' Gritty answered.

'That's a good idea,' Oriana said. 'All right with everyone?'

There was a murmur of approval.

'Do we have any volunteers?' she asked.

'I'll do it.' Grim-faced, Gritty was totally convincing. 'It'd be a privilege to damn the lot of them.'

'Me too,' Ralph called out.

'Ah. Two volunteers.' Oriana was clearly annoyed that Ralph had added an extra complication. 'How do we decide?'

Using Ralph's unimaginative nickname, Precious said, 'You're an old man, RH. I'm sorry to mention it like this, but you won't have long to live with … your burden. And if you got caught … Well, the powers-that-be can't do much to a man of your age.'

'Quite right,' he agreed, nodding.

'Anyone got anything else for us to think about?' Oriana asked.

'RH tends to let things out of the bag when he's talking to people,' Gritty said.

Ralph cackled and replied, 'That's true, Gritty.'

'We have a one-all draw.'

'I was first in the queue,' Gritty reminded them.

Troy sniffed and said, 'He's getting desperate.'

A different member of TRAPT called out, 'I'm persuaded by the age thing. I think RH should do it.'

'God's chosen one,' someone else agreed.

'Give me the vial,' Gritty said. 'I'll hold it out and RH can whack it with his stick.'

'It's a bit theatrical.' Oriana shrugged. 'But I like the idea of a joint effort.'

Gritty stood up. 'Let's get on with it.'

'Are you sure?' Oriana asked.

'Absolutely.'

Her eyes sought out Ralph. 'Are you sure as well?'

'Yes, definitely.' He made his way to the front.

Oriana looked at the two men, face to face, standing there as if about to fight an old-fashioned duel. 'This is it, then. No going back.'

They nodded at her.

'Let's take a few seconds for silent prayer.'

After half a minute, Oriana gave a little cough and held out the sealed container towards Gritty.

The undercover officer intended to enclose it in his large hand, leaving no glass for Ralph to strike, but the old man didn't wait. Impatient and unpredictable, he swung his stick immediately and with surprising force at Gritty's fist.

Gritty couldn't dodge quickly enough. Instead, he

tried to cushion the blow. Tried to soften it with his hand. The stick cracked him across the knuckles before he had the vial fully in his grip. He couldn't hold on and it shot out of his grasp.

They all turned. Every pair of eyes followed the vial as it flew up and across the room towards the door. It was a brief moment in time – a second, perhaps – but it seemed to happen in slow-motion.

The door opened and Troy, who had used the period of silent prayer to sprint into the building, dived towards the fearsome vessel. Outstretched, he slipped his right hand under the tumbling container and caught it centimetres above the floor.

Shaking with emotion, he got to his feet. Unable to trust himself with the vial, he gave it to Lexi who had appeared at his side. Together, they blocked the way to the exit.

'Stay exactly where you are,' Troy demanded. 'Don't try anything stupid. We've recorded this whole thing. You are all under arrest.' For a split-second, he glanced at Dominic but did not break his colleague's cover. He gave no hint that Gritty was anything other than a failed multiple murderer.

For the benefit of the inbuilt microphone in his life-logger, Troy said, 'Backup to the community centre. We need an immediate police escort. Ten to be arrested, questioned and charged.'

Lexi also sent a message. Hers went to Shallow
End Laboratories and Julia Neve Nineteen. 'One
unopened vial for immediate return to BSL4.'

SCENE 39

Saturday 19th April, Morning

On the way down the corridor, Troy and Lexi saw Dominic Varney emerging from the commander's office. He walked up to them and said, 'I've been explaining why I did what I did to Cheryl McVeigh. The new guy took it well.'

'Not surprising,' Troy replied. 'You gave him a clear run at the top job.'

'I guess.' He smiled and added, 'I pointed out the bugs while I was in there. I heaped praise on you two as well.'

'Did we need it?' Lexi asked.

'Probably not.'

Troy said, 'You did us a favour with TRAPT. Good work. Thanks.'

'Pleasure. Well, maybe not a pleasure. But between us, we got it sorted.'

'Yeah.'

He winked at them. 'See you around.'

'Mustn't keep the temporary commander waiting,' Lexi said with a mischievous smile. As she knocked on the door, she whispered to her partner, 'I'm looking forward to this.'

The commander looked up at them as if accusing them of ruining his plans for their murder investigation. 'Just when I'm about to appoint a new senior investigator, it seems that you two have closed the case.'

'Of course, we would have been able to do it earlier,' Lexi replied, 'but we were denied a search warrant for Fern Mountstephen's house.'

The police chief's eyes narrowed as he stared at her. 'I won't have insubordination for a perfectly rational – and legal – judgement, Lexi Four. In fact, I won't have insubordination for any reason.'

'Sorry,' she said, 'but you wouldn't understand. I'm an outer and, like every outer, I've been on this crippled plane that's about to crash. It's a relief when two young and inexperienced detectives come along and make it fly again.'

'I'm going to review the case before I make my report on you.'

'There's something else you should do first.'

'Is there?'

There was a knock at the door and Terabyte's long cute face appeared. 'You wanted a room debugging.'

'Yes,' the police chief replied. 'Come back in five minutes.'

As soon as Terabyte withdrew, the commander said to Lexi, 'You were about to enlighten me on what I should be doing.'

'Expecting an apology's probably too much,' she replied, 'but you should at least congratulate us for saving half of the human races.'

'I'm going to review the case before I ... '

'Huh. At least we're detectives, not temporary detectives.'

Lexi's usual composure had deserted her. Troy realized that, if there was a mark, his partner had just overstepped it. He was proud of her.

Her quip seemed to have an immediate effect on their boss. He did not attempt to retaliate. He simply waved them away. 'Dismissed. And ... '

They waited.

Reluctantly, the temporary commander said, 'I'm

pleased the case has come to a satisfactory conclusion.'

SCENE 40

Saturday 19th April, Noon

'Where are you taking me?' asked Troy.

'Home,' Lexi told him.

'*Your* home?'

'Yes.'

Troy frowned. 'What's on your mind?'

'Don't you know? Not perceptive enough?'

He shook his head.

'For saving every one of us,' Lexi said, 'you should be made an honorary outer.'

Troy laughed. 'No chance. Gran would murder me. Anyway, Dominic did it in the end.'

'It took his hand and yours.' Lexi turned into her

small, untidy garden and led Troy towards the door. 'To celebrate, I want to share lunch with you. And my friends.'

'Share? With your mates?' Troy grimaced. 'They'll make mincemeat of me.'

'Pardon?'

'They'll hate me.'

'True. But when I tell them you're the major who saved them all … we'll see.'

'Are you sure about this?'

They stepped into the porch. 'They ought to know. They need to have their prejudices shaken up.' She began to open the door.

'I might throw up when I see your food.'

'No you won't. Trust me.'

'Well … Grub, yes. But grubs, no.'

Lexi laughed. 'I've got the ideal thing. Some nice bread. Don't ask where the flour came from. And chocolate-mealworm spread.'

'Chocolate and mealworm? Combined?'

'For you and me, outer and major, it's perfect, isn't it?' She ushered him into the house.

Troy swallowed. 'Sounds … '

'Yummy?'

'Weird.' Troy took a deep breath and then smiled. 'But I'll give it a go.'

The real science behind the story

The crimes in all of *The Outer Reaches* books are inspired by genuine scientific issues and events. Here are a few details of the science that lies behind *Lethal Outbreak*.

Organisms from outer space

There is genuine concern about our ability to deal with alien bugs if they are ever found and brought back for study on Earth. They may be released by accident or design. If they turned out to be harmful, there would be serious consequences to the well-being of human civilizations. In the Earth's mild atmosphere, we simply don't know what it would take to kill bugs that might be hardened to the extreme extra-terrestrial conditions of a planet like Mars.

The outers' diet

While I have imagined a second human race called outers, I have not made up their diet. All of their meals are genuine bug-based food from around the world, eaten by more than two billion people. Eating insects and arachnids (entomophagy) is much better for the Earth's resources than eating meat. The global livestock trade emits more greenhouse gases than planes, trains and road vehicles combined. Replacing farm animals with protein-rich insects reduces the emissions enormously. Over 1,900 insect species are edible. There is even a conference called 'Insects to Feed the World' that promotes the use of insects as a human food.

Malcolm Rose is an established, award-winning author, noted for his gripping crime/thriller stories – all with a solid scientific basis.

Before becoming a full-time writer, Malcolm was a university lecturer and researcher in chemistry.

He says that chemistry and writing are not so different. *'In one life, I mix chemicals, stew them for a while and observe the reaction. In the other, I mix characters, stir in a bit of conflict and, again, observe the outcome.'*